BERSERK BY KENTARO MIURA
BERSERK © Kentaro Miura / Hakusensha, Inc.

BERSERK BY KENTARO MIURA

ベルセルク

BERSERK 37

BY
KENTARO MIURA
三浦建太郎

TRANSLATION
DUANE JOHNSON
LETTERING AND RETOUCH
REPLIBOOKS

DARK HORSE MANGA

PRESIDENT AND PUBLISHER
MIKE RICHARDSON

US EDITORS
CHRIS WARNER
FRED LUI

COLLECTION DESIGNER
DAVID NESTELLE

English-language version produced by
DARK HORSE COMICS and DIGITAL MANGA PUBLISHING.

BERSERK vol. 37 by KENTARO MIURA

Dark Horse Manga
A division of Dark Horse Comics LLC
10956 SE Main Street
Milwaukie OR 97222

DarkHorse.com

To find a comics shop in your area, go to comicshoplocator.com

First edition: November 2013

ISBN 978-1-61655-205-3

10 9 8
Printed in the United States of America

BERSERK

ベルセルク㊲

三浦建太郎

ガッツ *Guts*

The main character of the story, the Black Swordsman. He exists in the interstice, wears the Berserker armor, and his soul is constantly torn between protecting Casca and challenging Griffith. That struggle is nothing short of sublime.

キャスカ *Casca*

Former unit commander of the Band of the Hawk; mentally regressed from her experience in the eclipse. She now neither speaks nor conveys any feelings. Her brand, which reacts to evil, is narrowly shielded by Flora's talisman.

パック *Puck*

An elf who's long been with Guts on his journeys. His dust has the power to heal wounds. He confirmed that he's a wind spirit, and he also changes into Chestnut Puck.

イシドロ *Isidro*

Dreams of being the "ultimate swordsman," but his actual talent, not up to snuff, repeatedly endangers him. Nevertheless, the boy endeavors toward his dream. He is currently equipped with a fetish granted the protection of fire elementals.

シールケ *Schierke*

Disciple of Flora, witch of the spirit tree mansion. She supports Guts and the others through her use of magic; however, among her spells are some beyond her mastery, which occasionally place her in great peril as she tries to aid her allies. She has a stilted side to her personality.

グリフィス *Griffith*

Through the eclipse of the Crimson Behelit, he was reborn as Femto of the Godhand. Later he was incarnated in the imitation eclipse catalyzed by the egg-shaped apostle, thus returning to the physical world, in which he became the "absolute," without equal. He leads the reborn Band of the Hawk.

ファルネーゼ *Farnese*

Former commander of the Holy See's Holy Iron Chain Knights, and daughter of the Vandimion family, one of influential status and wealth in the religious sphere. She seeks to learn from Guts her own means of survival, and about the reality of the world.

セルピコ *Serpico*

Attendant of Farnese, and actually her brother. However, Farnese is not aware of the blood relationship. He is skilled in fighting, and currently clad in a fetish granted the protection of wind elementals.

リッケルト *Rickert*

A former member of the Band of the Hawk. As he was not involved in the eclipse, he does not have a brand. He became the apprentice of the blacksmith Godo and has made weapons for Guts to use.

イスマ *Isma*

A girl fisherman who lives on the island of the sea god. Treated like an outcast by the village there, she yearns for the outside world. Isma was actually a merrow all along, but she was not aware of this.

The sea god is on the move. Destroying the island as it emerges, the creature's form is beyond imagination. A school of merrow appear, surrounding the sea god. Their race has waged war on the sea god for many years. Among them is Isma's mother. Inside the sea god, Guts arrives at its heart while in his right mind and with Schierke's luminous body in tow, but the sound of the sea god's heartbeat is so loud, attacking it proves to be more difficult than Guts can handle.

ベルセルク 37

CONTENTS

FANTASIA ARC
ELF ISLAND CHAPTER

MERROW, PART 2 9

SIREN 31

SURFACING 55

SHOOTING STAR 79

SPRING FLOWERS OF DISTANT DAYS, PART 1 105

SPRING FLOWERS OF DISTANT DAYS, PART 2 129

SPRING FLOWERS OF DISTANT DAYS, PART 3 153

COVERED WAGON 179

PARADISE 205

幻造世界〈ファンタジア〉篇／妖精島の章

人魚(メロウ)②

MERROW, PART 2

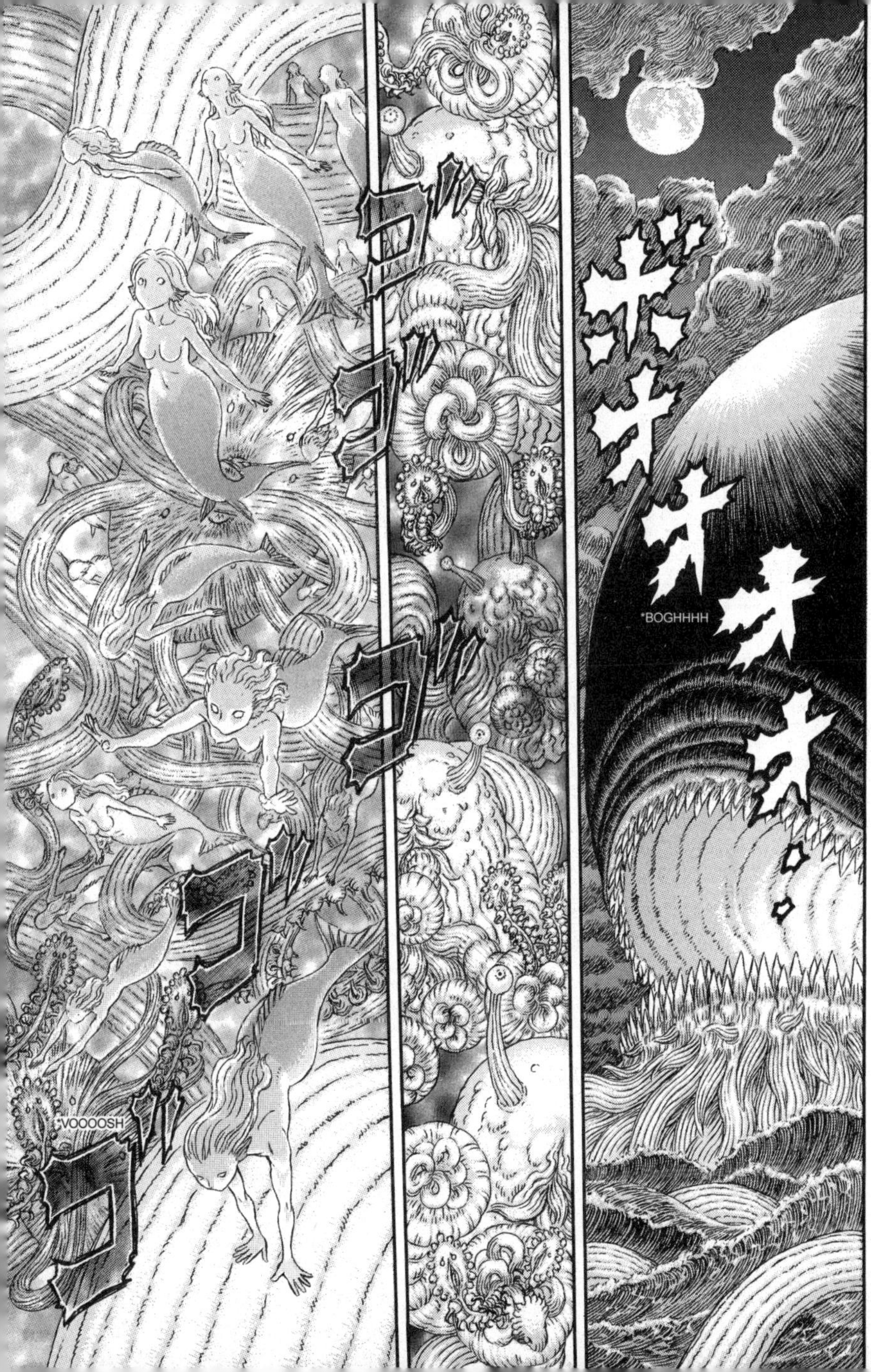
*BOGHHHH
*VOOOOSH

TARGET THAT HUGE LEVIATHAN!
COM-MENCE BOM-BARD-MENT!
LET 'EM HAVE IT!!
*FX: BOOM BOOM

*BOGHHH
LISTEN TO IT WAIL!
IT'S HURTIN', IT'S HURTIN'!
DIRECT HIT, ALL SHOTS!
THE SEA AND THE CLOUDS HAVE BEGUN TO SWIRL AROUND IT.
LOOK AT THAT, CAPTAIN.
!
*BDMMM
IT MEANS TO DRAG US IN.
*FX: ZHMMM
CONVENIENT ENOUGH. WE'LL USE THE WIND AND WHIRLPOOL TO SHOW IT HOW A CIRCLING BOMBARD-MENT'S DONE.
WE WILL, AYE.

Y-YOU'RE EXAGGER-ATING...
SHIELD OF THE GODDESS, INDEED. YOU'RE INCREDIBLE, FARNESE.
HEH! WE'RE HAVIN' A TENTACLE COOKOUT TONIGHT!
*FX: SLURP
*BWOOOSH
*ZHM
*ZHM
*ZHM
HEY!
LOOK OUT, OR YOU'LL BE BACK IN THE DRINK...
*FX: DOOOOSH
GUTS ...
IS ISMA OKAY DOWN THERE IN THIS ROUGH SEA?
*SHOMMM

I CAN BREATHE UNDER WATER!
AWESOME!
LOOK HOW FREELY I CAN SWIM!!
AND I CAN TALK!
I COULD CATCH ALL THE FISH LIKE THIS!
ZOOM
*SWIP
*KROSSSH
YES!
*HYNN
*HYNN

HEHEH! YOU KNOW, IF ANYTHING...
...MAYBE I REALLY HAVE TURNED INTO A FISH.
BUT HOW THE HECK...
...DO THEY ALL PLAN TO BEAT SUCH A HUGE THING?
*FX: FWOOMP
UH OH...!

*SWAY
?!
*SWAY
*GRAB
*ZHMMM
*SHOOM
WOWWW!!
A REAL MERROW!
Y--
YOU SAVED ME.
UM...
WHAT'D YOU JUST DO...?
I SANG.
MERROWS FIGHT USING SONG.
HER VOICE...

WELCOME HOME...
...ISMA.
...
...MAAA...

*DSSSH
*BOOOM
THAT SOUND IS... CANNON FIRE.
GUTS!
DO YOU HEAR THAT?! IT'S A BOM-BARDMENT!
THE OTHERS ARE STILL SAFE!

*GCHAK
GOT-CHA...
WELL, THEN...
WE'D BETTER HURRY.
SCHIERKE, ARE THERE ANY LITTLE FISH LEFT?
WHERE'S THE HEART?
GUTS...
YOU MEAN...
...YOU CAN'T SEE OR HEAR...?

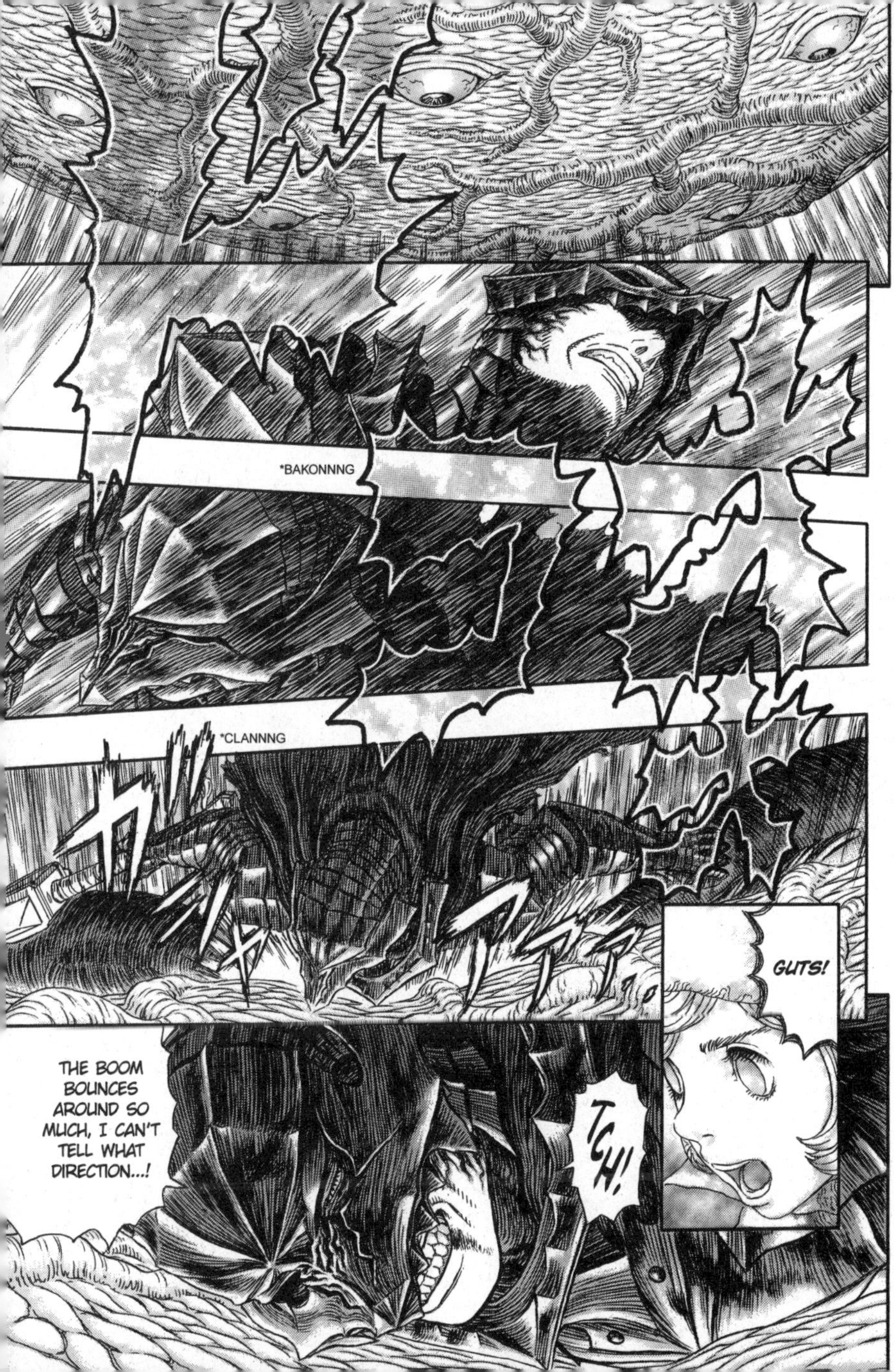
*BAKONNNG
*CLANNNG
GUTS!
THE BOOM BOUNCES AROUND SO MUCH, I CAN'T TELL WHAT DIRECTION...!
TCH!

YOU FINISHED OFF ALL THE FISH MONSTERS.
BUT...
...ALL YOU HAVE TO DO NOW IS STRIKE THE HEART WITH YOUR SWORD...
EVEN IF HE IS WEARING THE BERSERKER ARMOR...
THERE'S NO DEFENSE AGAINST THAT BOOMING PULSE. HE CAN'T TAKE ANY MORE...
JUST GET CLOSE AND SLASH IT, HUH?
...
...
...
THAT'S GOOD. SOUNDS EASIER THAN A FOOL'S ERRAND.
I THINK I CAN HOBBLE MY WAY THERE.
GUIDE ME IN THE RIGHT DIRECTION. IT'LL BE LIKE BLIND MAN'S BLUFF.
OKAY!
FOR-WARD, SLIGHTLY TO THE RIGHT...
*GCHAK
*BA
*KONG

*GRIND
FIVE MORE STEPS...
*GAHAH!
*CHFF
*KONNNG
*CLANNG
*WHUP
*SHANG
GUTS...!!

THIS DAMN THING'S *RATTLED.*
THE PULSE KEEPS GETTING FASTER.
YOU CAN'T...
...*TAKE* ANY MORE...!
WE'RE THE ONES WHO...
...HAVE IT CORNERED.

*CLANNNG
GUTS
....!

TCH...!
NONE OF MY SENSES ARE WORKING.
MY WHOLE BODY'S NUMB...
...AND IT'S LIKE MY ARMS AND LEGS ARE GONE.
....
WHAT DO I DO?

IS THAT...
...SINGING?

幻造世界〈ファンタジア〉篇／妖精島の章

声連（セイレン）

SIREN

THE SEA GOD'S FLOUNDER-ING?!
WHAT?!

*BOGAHHHHH
*ZHMM
*ZHMM
*ZHMM
*ZHMM
*ZHMM
*FX: BROHNNN
*FX: GOOOOSH
IT JUST SPIT SOMETHING OUT! REMINDS ME OF A WHALE BLOWING.
THAT BASTARD'S IN SOME MAJOR DISTRESS.
IT SEEMS THAT WAY.
THERE'S SINGING.

I HEAR SINGING...
...COMING FROM THE SEA.

IS THIS...
...MERROWS SINGING?!
AMAZING!
IT'S ECHOING ALL OVER THE PLACE...
THE SEA GOD...
...IS TREMBLING!!
*OHHHHHN

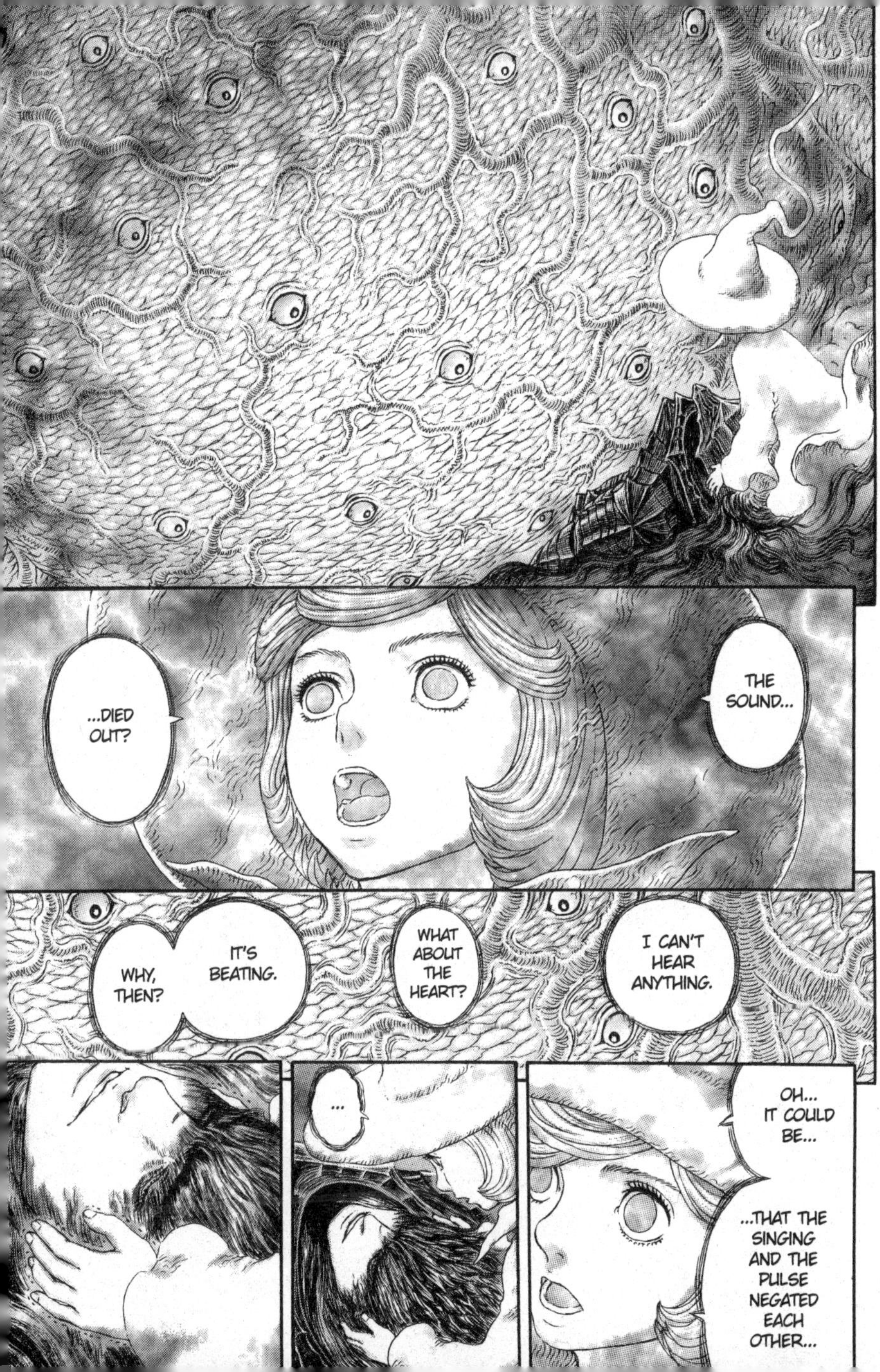
THE SOUND...
...DIED OUT?
I CAN'T HEAR ANYTHING.
WHAT ABOUT THE HEART?
IT'S BEATING.
WHY, THEN?
OH... IT COULD BE...
...THAT THE SINGING AND THE PULSE NEGATED EACH OTHER...
...

COME ON!
YOU NEED TO STAND UP, GUTS!
THIS IS YOUR CHANCE TO FINISH IT OFF, NOW THAT THE PULSE IS SILENCED!
DON'T WE HAVE IT CORNERED?!
IF THAT WASN'T JUST BRAVADO...
THEN PLEASE, GET UP AND DO THIS!
...HEH!
YOU SAID IT.
HEY...

I KNOW...
YOU HAVEN'T HAD YOUR FILL YET.
THIS IS PRETTY LAZY, SEEING AS YOU ALWAYS TALK SUCH A BIG GAME.
QUIT LAYIN' DOWN ON THE JOB.
GET UP AND PIERCE SOME FLESH AND BONE.
LET ME FEEL THE PAIN.

ザク
*CHNK
ザク
*CHNK
ザク
*CHNK
ザク
*CHNK

GUTS...!!
WHICH WAY?!
STRAIGHT AHEAD...!! KEEP GOING...
NOW!

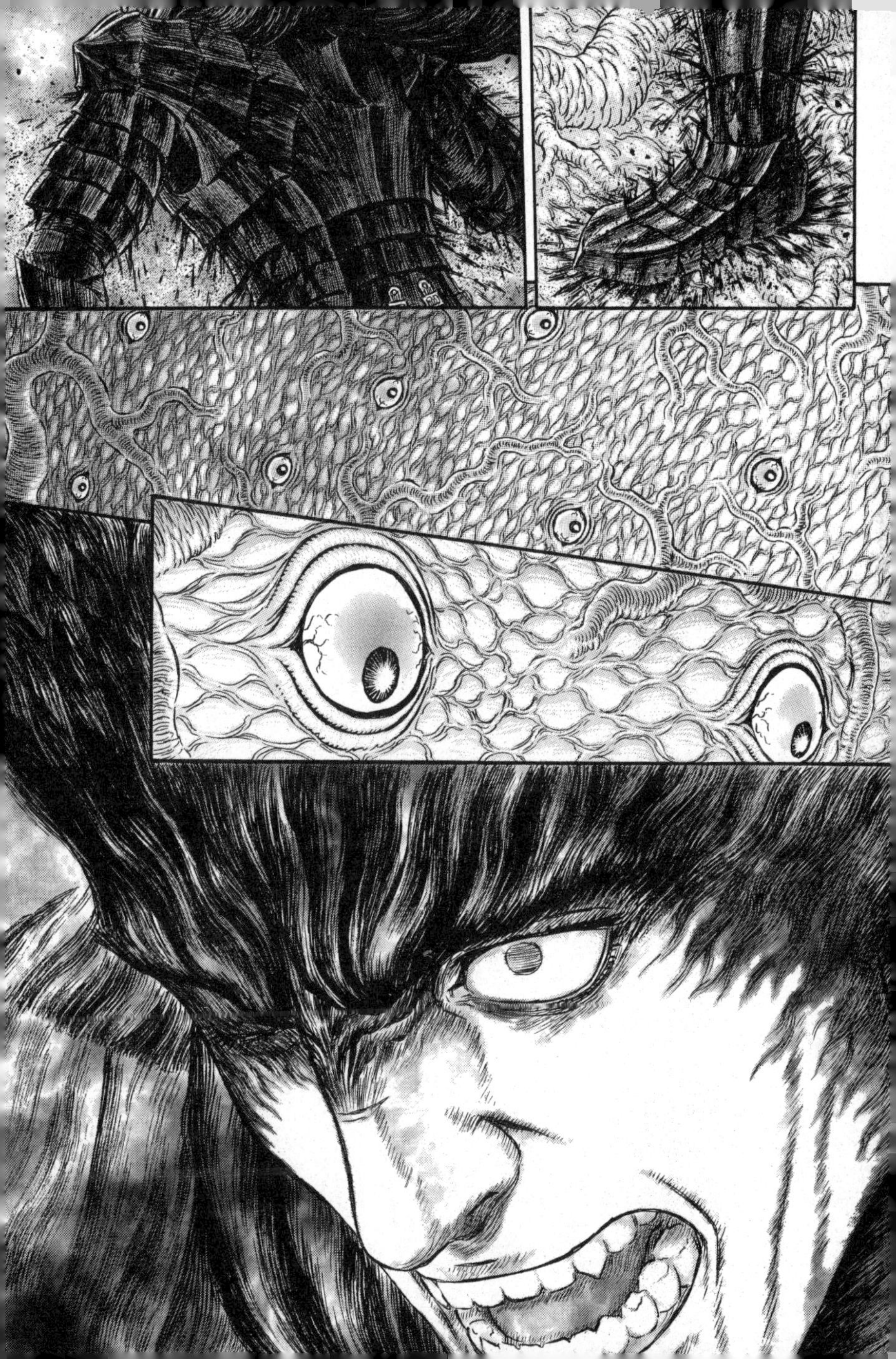

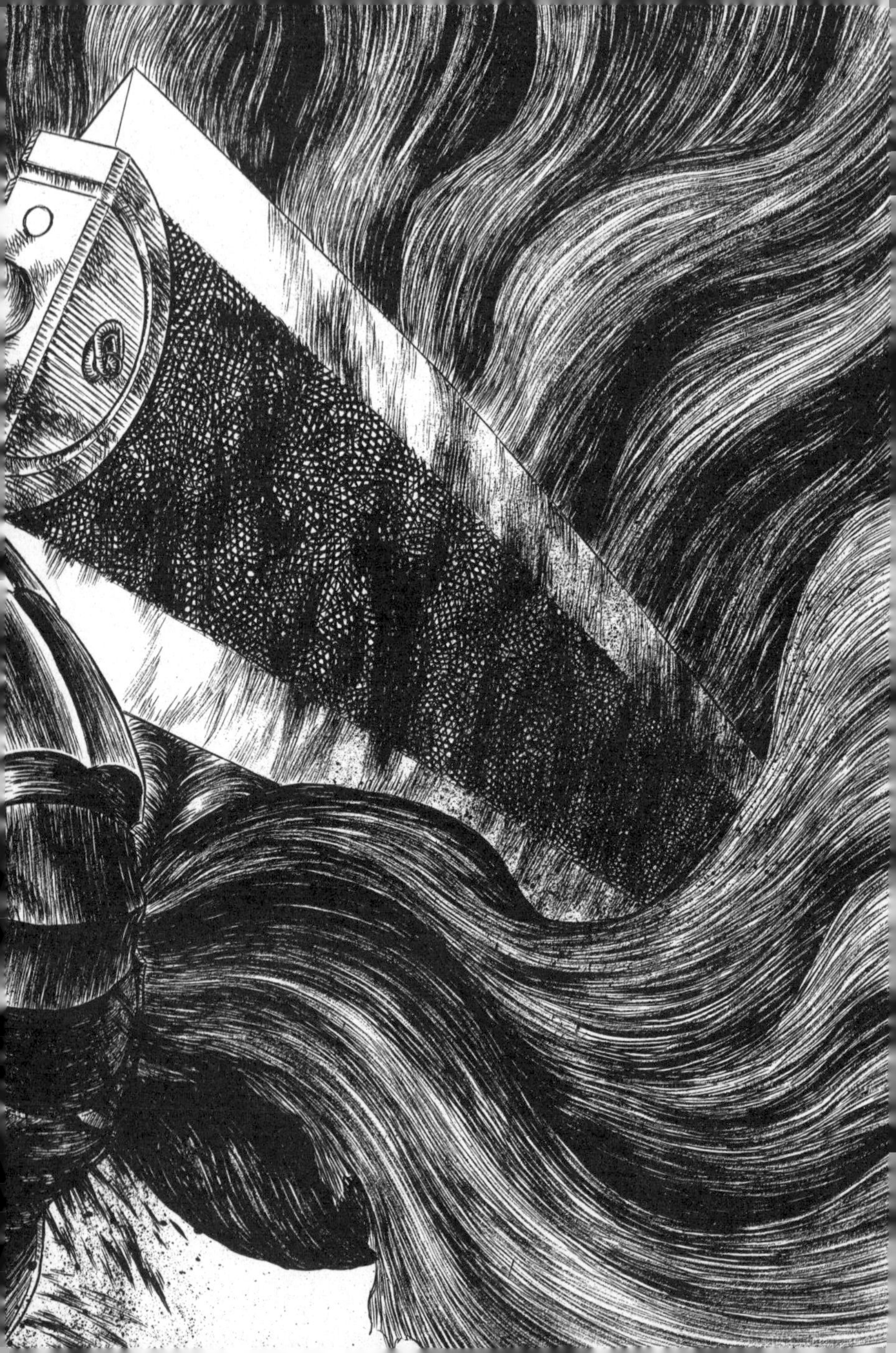

YOU DID IT...!!
*BWOOOOOSH

*BWOLLLMF

*DOOSH
*DOOSH
*DOOSH
PUKE BOMBIN' RAID! GRODY.
NOW IT'S SPOUTING OUT SHIPS! IS THIS SOME ATTACK?!
WHAT THE --?!
!
THE SEA GOD...
ゴボボ
*GOLLLB
IT'S COLLAPS-ING...?!

IS IT... ...DEAD?
IT... ...SEEMS THAT WAY.
UHAH!
WE DID IT!
THE SEA GOD IS HISTORY!
*ROHHHHHHH

MISTRESS!
SCHIERKE!
!
HNN...
TELL US WHERE THE HELL YOU WERE AND WHAT YOU DID! WHERE'S GUTS?
......
I SEE YOU'RE SAFE.
OH, NO...
?
GUTS...
GUTS IS...

幻造世界〈ファンタジア〉篇／妖精島の章

浮上

SURFACING

HURRY...
PLEASE HURRY AND BRING THE SHIP CLOSE TO THE SEA GOD!
GUTS IS...
THAT'S WHERE...
...HE IS STILL...
HEY...
SCHIERKE?
...
COME ON, DON'T SCARE US.
THAT MONSTER'S KICKED THE BUCKET, RIGHT? THERE'S NOTHIN' TO WORRY ABOUT.
GUTS IS CERTI-FIED TOUGH.

GUTS IS...
...INSIDE THE SEA GOD.
HE'S HURT BADLY...
AND HE CANNOT EVEN MOVE AT THIS POINT...
WE MANAGED TO INVADE ITS BODY TOGETHER...
...AND WE RUPTURED ITS HEART.
YOU DID WHAT?
HELL, THAT'S AS EXTREME AS EVER.
FIGURES GUTS WOULD BE THE ONE TA KILL IT.
...
BUT JUST THEN, WE WERE ENGULFED BY THE BLOOD THAT GUSHED OUT...
AND THE IMPACT KNOCKED ME LOOSE FROM HIM...
HURRY!
WE HAVE TO FIND HIM, OR ELSE...!

BUT AS IT WAS DYING, IT SPOUTED OUT A LARGE AMOUNT OF BLOODY VOMIT.
PERHAPS GUTS IS SOMEWHERE AMONGST IT...
!
NO, HE IS NOT.
*BLACH
*BLACH
HEYA!
WE DID IT!
MER-ROW...
ISMA! YOU'RE ALL RIGHT!

UM... WHO MIGHT YOU BE?
OTHER THAN YOU, THERE ARE NO SIGNS OF HUMANS AROUND THE SEA GOD.
EHE-HE-HEH...
SHE'S MY MA.
FIRST, ON BEHALF OF OUR ENTIRE SEA TRIBE...
...I THANK YOU HEROIC SAILORS FOR FIGHTING ALONG-SIDE US.

THANK YOU.
TH-THAT IS MOST THOUGHTFUL OF YOU.
*BOW
AU
THANK YOU.
*BOW
*BOW
I LISTENED TO YOUR CONVERSATION.
AS THE YOUNG LADY THERE SAID...
...IF YOUR COMRADE IS STILL ALIVE, HE IS PROBABLY STILL INSIDE THE SEA GOD'S BODY.
IT IS BEGINNING TO SINK.
IT WOULD THEREFORE BE BEST TO HURRY.
THAT IS NOT ALL, EITHER.
MANY OF THE SEA DRAGONS IN THIS REGION...
...WILL CATCH THE SCENT OF THE DISGORGED BLOOD AND LIKELY SOON DESCEND UPON THE SEA GOD TO CONSUME ITS PUTRID FLESH.
IS IT OVER?
READY A CUTTER!
WE'LL ROW ALONGSIDE THAT THING!
I'M COMING WITH!

WE WILL ASSIST YOU.
FELLING THE SEA GOD WAS OUR TRIBE'S...
NO, IT WAS THE DEAREST WISH OF ALL THAT LIVE IN THIS REGION OF THE OCEAN.
IT WAS THANKS TO YOU THAT WE MANAGED IT.
PLEASE LET US HELP.
BY ALL MEANS!
PLEASE DO!
WE'RE ON IT!!
*PLASH

MISTRESS, I WILL SEARCH FOR GUTS USING MY LUMINOUS BODY...
YOU MUSTN'T!
WE DO NOT KNOW WHEN THE SEA DRAGONS WILL ARRIVE.
FARNESE, YOU MUST CONTINUE TO MAINTAIN YOUR SPELL.
YES, BUT...
I WILL GO AGAIN...
HEY ...!
SCHIERKE!
*STAGGER
M-MISTRESS!
PLEASE DO NOT PUSH TOO HARD!
SHE'S RIGHT! YOU'VE DONE THAT ENOUGH FOR ONE DAY!
BUT, THIS IS MY RESPONSIBILITY...
JUST GET SOME REST, ALREADY! SHOWOFF!
YOU'RE GONNA MAKE ME LOOK BAD IF YA KEEP SUCCEEDIN'!

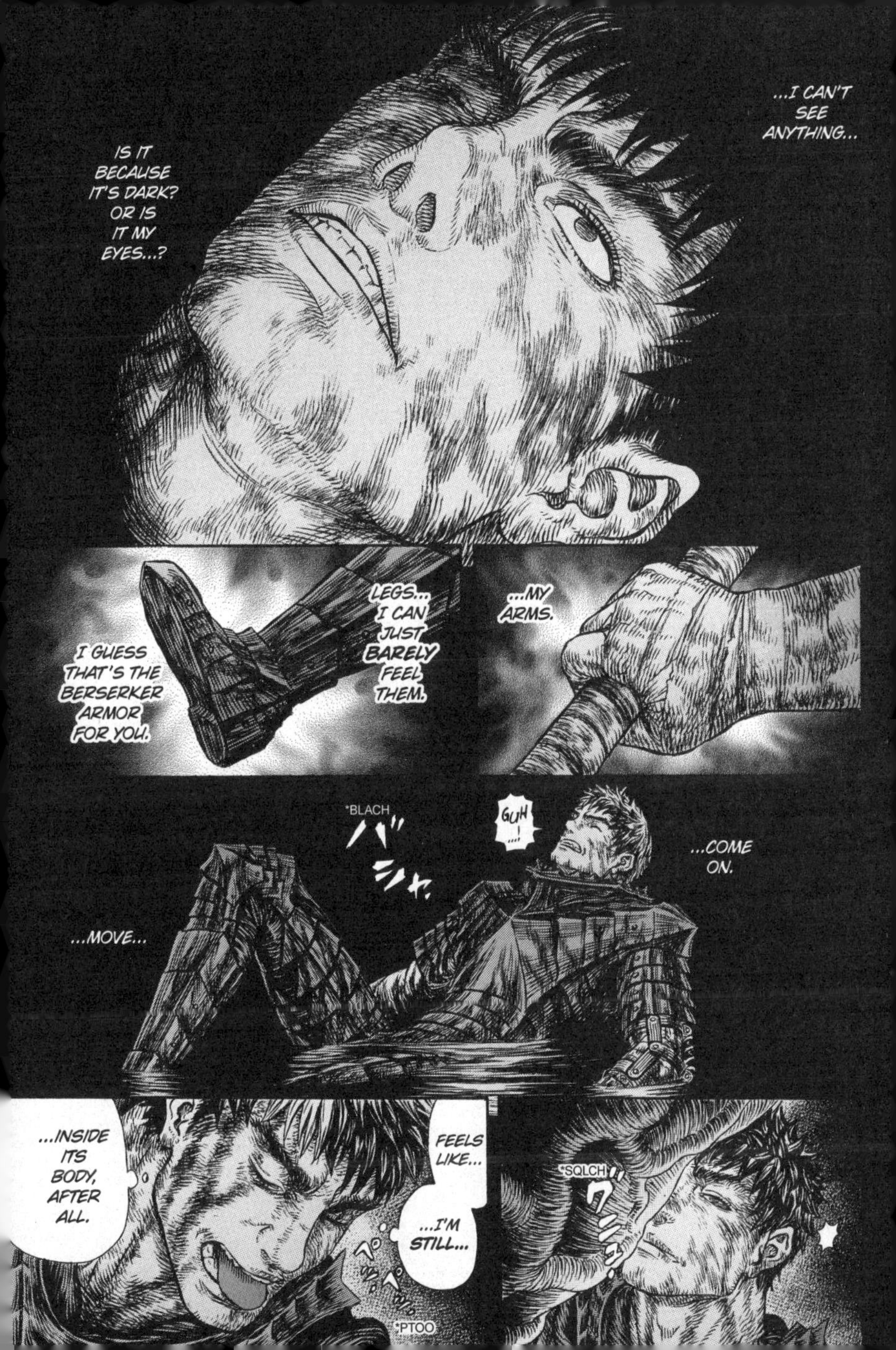
...I CAN'T SEE ANYTHING...
IS IT BECAUSE IT'S DARK? OR IS IT MY EYES...?
...MY ARMS.
LEGS... I CAN JUST BARELY FEEL THEM.
I GUESS THAT'S THE BERSERKER ARMOR FOR YOU.
...COME ON.
GUH!
*BLACH
...MOVE...
*SQLCH
FEELS LIKE...
...I'M STILL...
...INSIDE ITS BODY, AFTER ALL.
*PTOO

HEY!
SCHIER-KE.
...
...
... NOTHING.
I GUESS SHE GOT PULLED OFF ENTIRELY.
LOOKS LIKE THOUGHT TRANSFERENCE DOESN'T WORK FROM INSIDE HERE, EITHER.
THIS OCTOPUS IS TROUBLE EVEN WHEN IT'S DEAD.
AT LEAST I KNOW WHICH WAY IS UP.
*POKE
*FWOOSH
*BLACH
IT'S HARD TO BREATHE.
CRAP, I'VE GOT TO HURRY AND GET OUT OF HERE.
SO ALL I CAN DO IS KEEP CUTTING MY WAY UPWARDS WITH THIS...
WHOA ...!
*OOOOOSH

SHIT!
I BLED THIS THING OUT, AND THERE'S STILL THIS MUCH?!
IS THIS IT?!
HERE, IN THIS MUCK...
... ...
IS THIS HOW IT ENDS?!

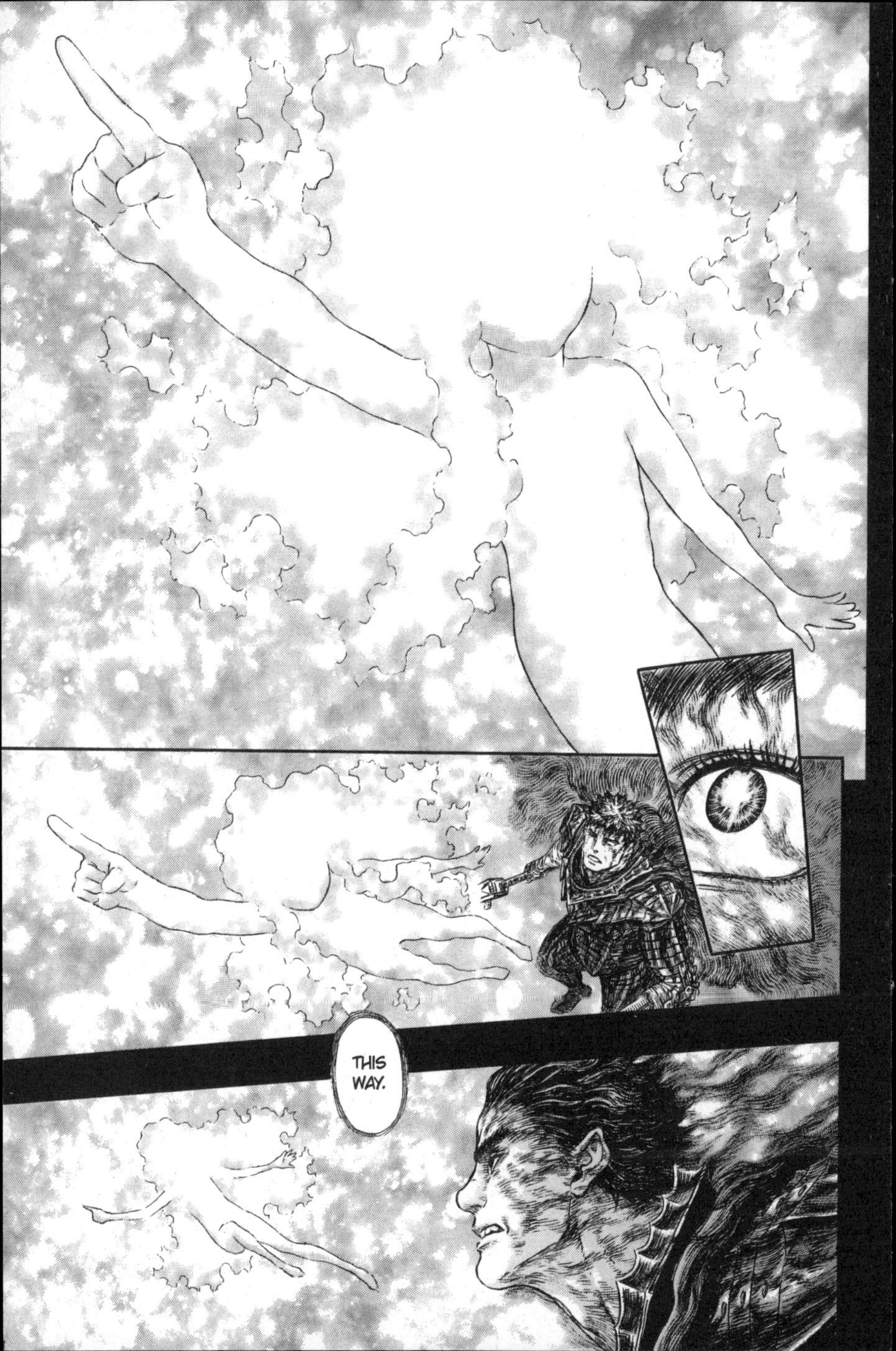
THIS WAY.

CAPTAIN, YOU NEEDN'T GO YOURSELF.
AH! HEY NOW, LAD!
ALL HANDS, JUST SIT TIGHT.
YOU HEARD HIM.
UGH! WHAT A BLOODY STINK!
I CAN HARDLY STAND IT!
THERE'S SO MUCH SPACE IN HERE. I CAN'T EVEN SEE THE REAR.
*PLOOSH
WHAT IF IT BITES DOWN FROM RIGOR MORTIS?
DON'T SAY THAT STUFF NOW.
WE ELVES CAN JUST SLIP THROUGH THE CRACKS. ♡
HOYYY! BOSS GUTS!
GUUUTS! YOU ALIVE ?!

WELL?
NO-THIN'.
WE DON'T SENSE HIM.
MAYBE HE'S DEEPER IN.
THOUGHT TRANSFERENCE ISN'T REACHING HIM, EITHER.
HAVE YOU GUYS FOUND HIM?
NO. WHAT ABOUT YOU?!
RIGHT NOW EVERYBODY'S BOUNCING SOUND AROUND...
...TO SEARCH INSIDE THE BODY.
NOT THAT I REALLY GET IT.
*TONNN
*TONNN
*FX: TONNN

*SHAAAAA
UH OH!
CAP-TAIN!
WE CAN'T REMAIN HERE!
LET'S CAST OFF!
QUICK-LY!
BEFORE WE GET DRAGGED DOWN WITH IT!
*SHAAAAA
Y-YEAH, BUT CAN WE JUST LEAVE?!
DON'T MAKE THIS ANY HARDER.
GET MOVIN', FISH FOOD.
WE DON'T HAVE ANY CHOICE! LET THE MERROWS HANDLE IT!
*FX: HEFT
*DZHHHH
... GUTS.

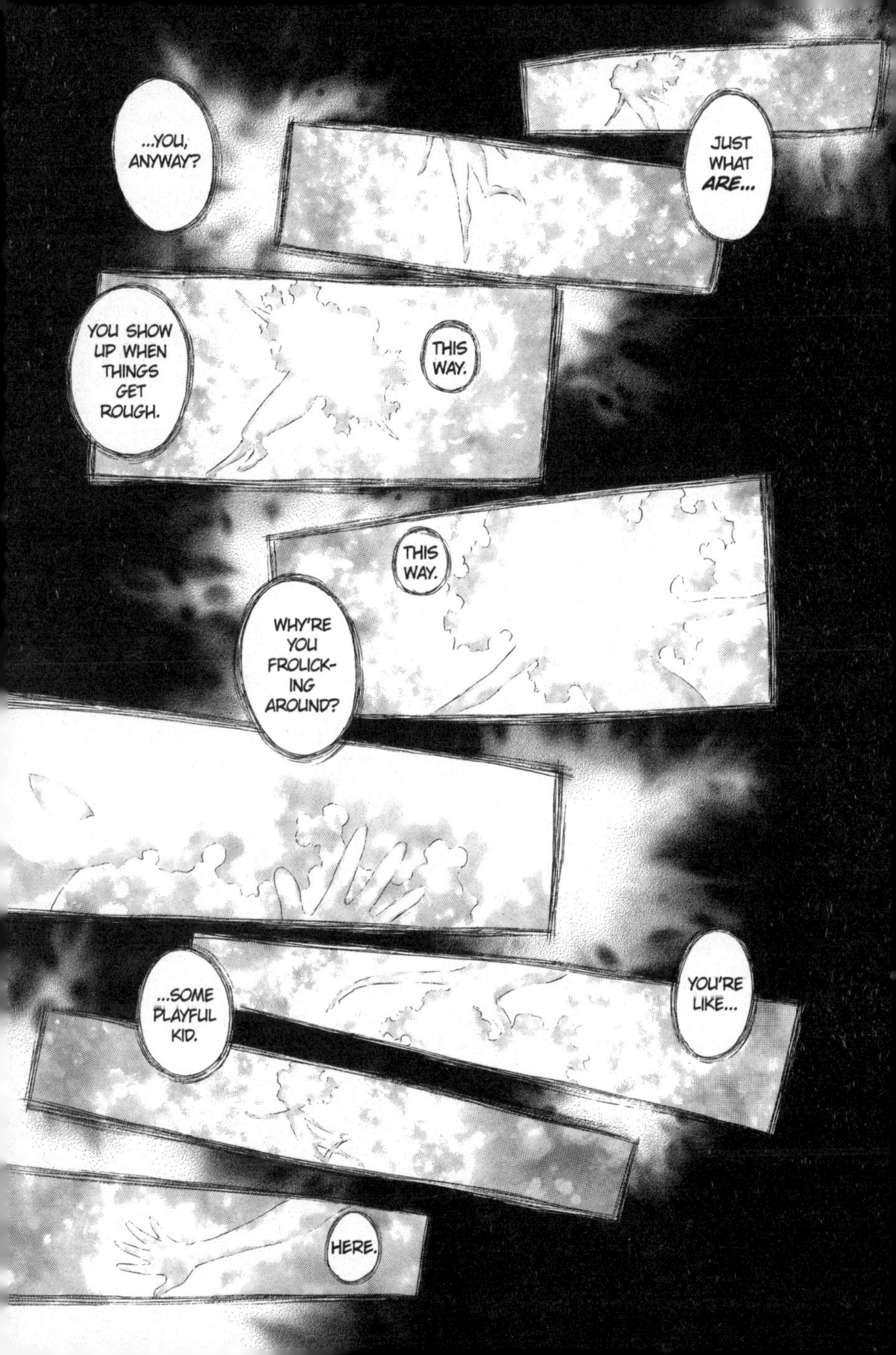
JUST WHAT ARE...
...YOU, ANYWAY?
THIS WAY.
YOU SHOW UP WHEN THINGS GET ROUGH.
THIS WAY.
WHY'RE YOU FROLICK-ING AROUND?
YOU'RE LIKE...
...SOME PLAYFUL KID.
HERE.

*BLOOOOSH
...SEA-WATER?!
THAT'S OUT-SIDE!!
...!

AUUU...

幻造世界〈ファンタジア〉篇／妖精島の章

流星

SHOOTING STAR

*ZHAAAAA
*BDOOOOSH

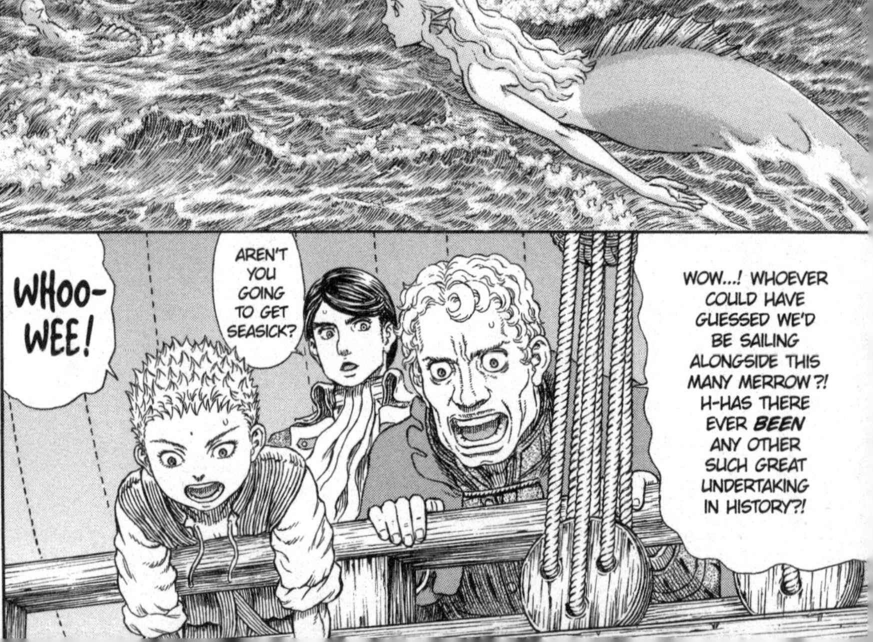
WOW...! WHOEVER COULD HAVE GUESSED WE'D BE SAILING ALONGSIDE THIS MANY MERROW?! H-HAS THERE EVER BEEN ANY OTHER SUCH GREAT UNDERTAKING IN HISTORY?!
AREN'T YOU GOING TO GET SEASICK?
WHOO-WEE!

I NEVER EXPECTED THEY'D VOLUNTEER TO GUIDE US TO ELF ISLAND.
NYA HA HAH
IT MUST BE BECAUSE YOU'RE SAILING ON THE *SEAHORSE*, ISMA.

NAH, THAT'S NOT IT! IT'S FOR HELPING OUT WITH TAKING DOWN THE SEA GOD.
THAT'S WHAT MA SAID.
HUH?
BUT WHAT ABOUT YOU?
YOU FINALLY MET YOUR MA, RIGHT?
WOULDN'T YOU RATHER BE IN THE WATER?
JUST YOU AND HER... AND ALL THE OTHER MERROWS.
... HNNN
I'D FEEL...
...KINDA EMBARRASSED.
FOR NOW, I'M MORE COMFORT-ABLE UP HERE WITH YOU GUYS!
*WHAP *WHAP
O-KAY...
BY THE WAY, WHERE'S SCHIERKE AND EVERYONE ELSE?
OH. CASCA AND THE KID ARE TIRED, SO THEY'RE SLEEPING IN A CABIN.

IS-IS HE OKAY? HE GOT REALLY BANGED UP.
IT'S ALWAYS LIKE THAT AFTER A BIG BATTLE.
SCHIERKE, FARNY, AND THE OTHERS ARE TAKING CARE OF GUTS.
THEY WORK US TO THE BONE EVERY SINGLE TIME.
UH... IS THIS CORRECT?
YES.
BY HOLDING YOUR HANDS UP TO HIS WOUNDS THAT WAY, YOU CIRCULATE YOUR FLOW OF OD WITH HIS, THUS BOOSTING HIS HEALING POWER.
IS THAT A V FOR VIC-TORY?
GUTS, CAN YOU SEE ME?
GOOD...
*WHEW
YOU ACCOMPLISHED THAT RITUAL...
...SO YOU SHOULD BE READY TO MANIPULATE A BIT OF OD FLOW.
YES, I DO...
...FEEL IT.

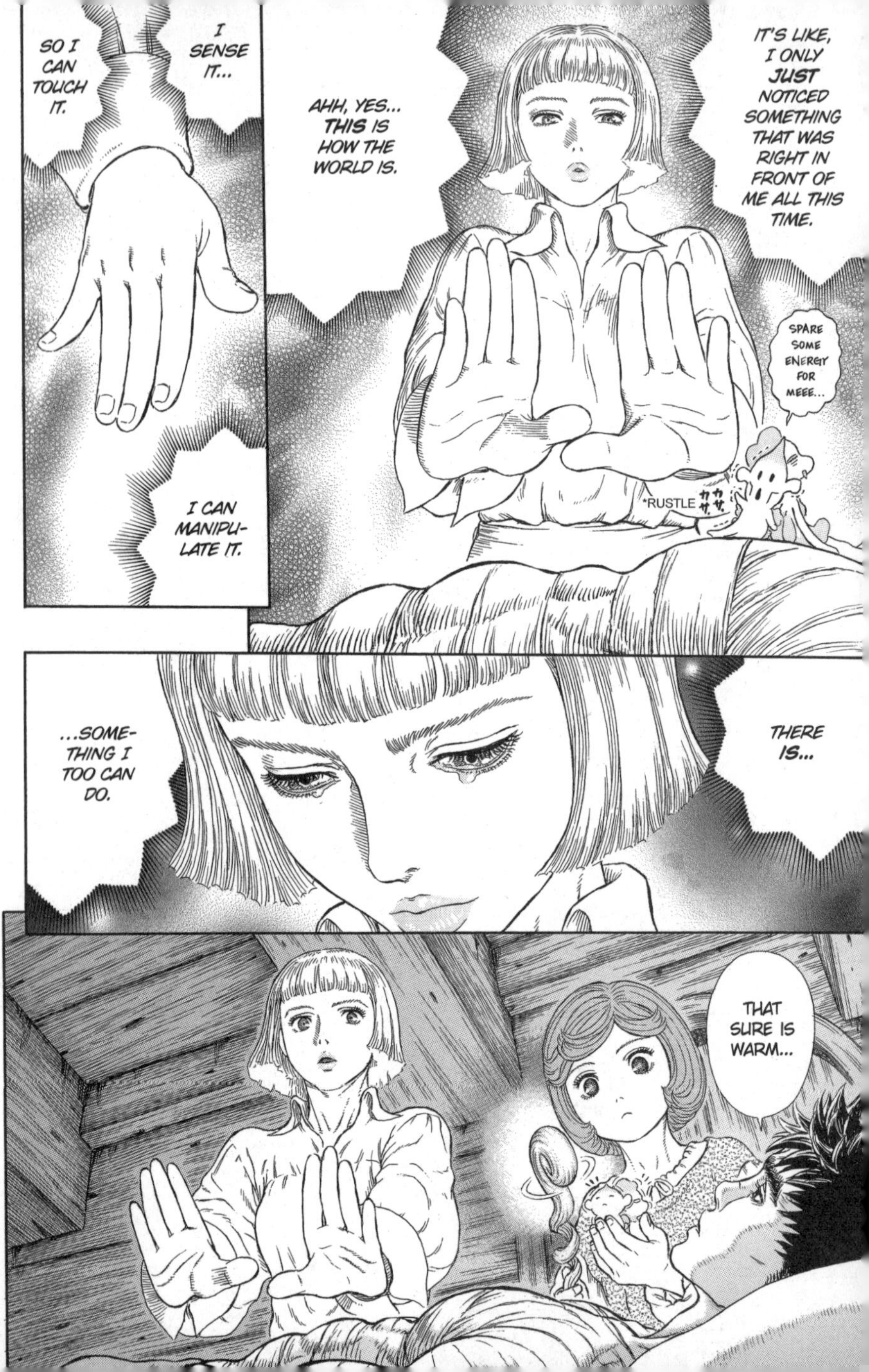
IT'S LIKE, I ONLY JUST NOTICED SOMETHING THAT WAS RIGHT IN FRONT OF ME ALL THIS TIME.
AHH, YES... THIS IS HOW THE WORLD IS.
SPARE SOME ENERGY FOR MEEE...
*RUSTLE
カサ カサ
I SENSE IT...
SO I CAN TOUCH IT.
I CAN MANIPULATE IT.
THERE IS...
...SOMETHING I TOO CAN DO.
THAT SURE IS WARM...

IT MAKES IT EASY TO FORGET HOW COLD I JUST FELT, LIKE I WAS STILL UNDERWATER.
YOU'RE GREAT AT THIS, FARNESE.
...YOU'RE WELCOME.
RIGHT NOW, MY WARMTH...
IT'S CLOBBERIN' TIME!
RE-FRESH.
...IS FLOWING INTO AND AROUND WITHIN YOU.
...
...
...

......
*KREEE
AUUU
OO OOOO
IS SOME-THING WRONG?
WELL ...

AHHH
NNAHHH
WHAT'S GOING ON?
!
CASCA!
OH OH
WHAT COULD IT BE?
*TURN
*TURN
SHE SEEMS TO BE SEARCHING FOR SOME-THING.
NO! YOU MUSTN'T GET UP YET...
Natural Born NEET
I DON'T WANNA WORK ANYMORE.
YOU'RE BAD FOR MY SKIN!
YEAH, BUT...
OOOO...

...
...
...
A-ANYWAY, GUTS, YOU GET SOME REST. I'LL MANAGE WITH HER SOMEHOW.
AHHHH
YOU WOULD JUST GET HER MORE AND MORE ADDLED...
UM ... I MEAN ...
SORRY.
I'LL LEAVE HER TO YOU.
...ALL RIGHT.
OHHHH

!
*POKE
I KNOW WHY CASCA'S CARRYIN' ON.
Y'KNOW THAT BLACK-HAIRED BOY?
HE'S GONE.
THERE'S NO SIGN OF HIM ANYWHERE, SIR.
WE SEARCHED EVERYWHERE, FROM CROW'S NEST TO HOLD...
BUT WE'RE TALKING ABOUT A CHILD. I THINK CURIOSITY TOOK OVER, AND HE SLIPPED INTO SOME NOOK SOMEWHERE.
ANY LUCK ON YOUR END, MISS WITCH?
NO, NO-THING.

IF HE IS NOT ON BOARD...
...THAT MEANS...
I RECALL HIS OD...
BUT I CANNOT PERCEIVE IT ANYWHERE ON THIS SHIP.
DON'T TELL ME HE FELL OVER-BOARD...
YEAH...
BUT WOULDN'T THAT BE WEIRD?
THERE ARE MERROW SWIMMING ALL AROUND THE SHIP.
IF SOMEONE FELL IN, THEY'D BE SURE TO NOTICE, AND I KNOW THEY WOULDN'T IGNORE HIM.
...THAT'S TRUE.
SO WHERE THE HELL DID HE GO?
TELE-PORT?
DID HE JUST VANISH IN A PUFF OF SMOKE?
THE SAME THING HAPPENED BEFORE.
THE TIME WE FIRST MET THAT BOY...
OH, YOU'RE RIGHT.
IT WAS A NIGHT WITH A FULL MOON, JUST LIKE THIS.

THE FULL MOON IS WHEN MAGICAL FORCES ARE AT THEIR STRONGEST.
IT'S THE NIGHT WHEN THOSE ASSOCIATED WITH THE ASTRAL WORLD, SUCH AS GOBLINS AND ELVES, RUN RAMPANT.
ON TWO SUCH NIGHTS NOW, HE'S SUDDENLY APPEARED BEFORE US, THEN VANISHED BEFORE WE KNEW IT...
AND THIS TIME, IT WAS ON A REMOTE, SOLITARY ISLAND, THEN ONBOARD A SHIP. I THINK THIS HAS GONE BEYOND THE REALM OF COINCIDENCE.
THEN, WHAT?
YOU'RE SAYIN' HE'S...
...A GOBLIN OR SOME-THIN'?
HIS OD CERTAINLY WAS DIFFERENT FROM THAT OF HUMANS, IN SOME RESPECT.
BUT HE DOES NOT SEEM TO BE THAT TYPE OF REPULSIVE BEING. HE DIDN'T CAUSE US ANY HARM EITHER...
AS YOU KNOW, HE WAS QUITE ATTACHED TO CASCA.
OHHHH
WELL, WHAT IS HE, THEN?
THIS IS CONJEC-TURE ON MY PART...

BUT HE MIGHT BE AN EMISSARY FROM ELF ISLAND, COME TO INVESTIGATE US...
IS SUCH A THING POSSIBLE, THOUGH? THEY SHOULDN'T BE AWARE OF US THERE...
IT SEEMS THAT AMONG THE ELVES, SOME HAVE GREAT POWERS...
...THAT ALLOW THEM TO DECIPHER FATES THAT TRANSCEND TIME, AND TO USE HIDDEN, SECRET PATHS TO CROSS GREAT DISTANCES.
IT'S POSSIBLE THAT BOY IS NO MERE EMISSARY...
...BUT RATHER...
...A MANIFESTATION OF THE FLOWER STORM MONARCH.

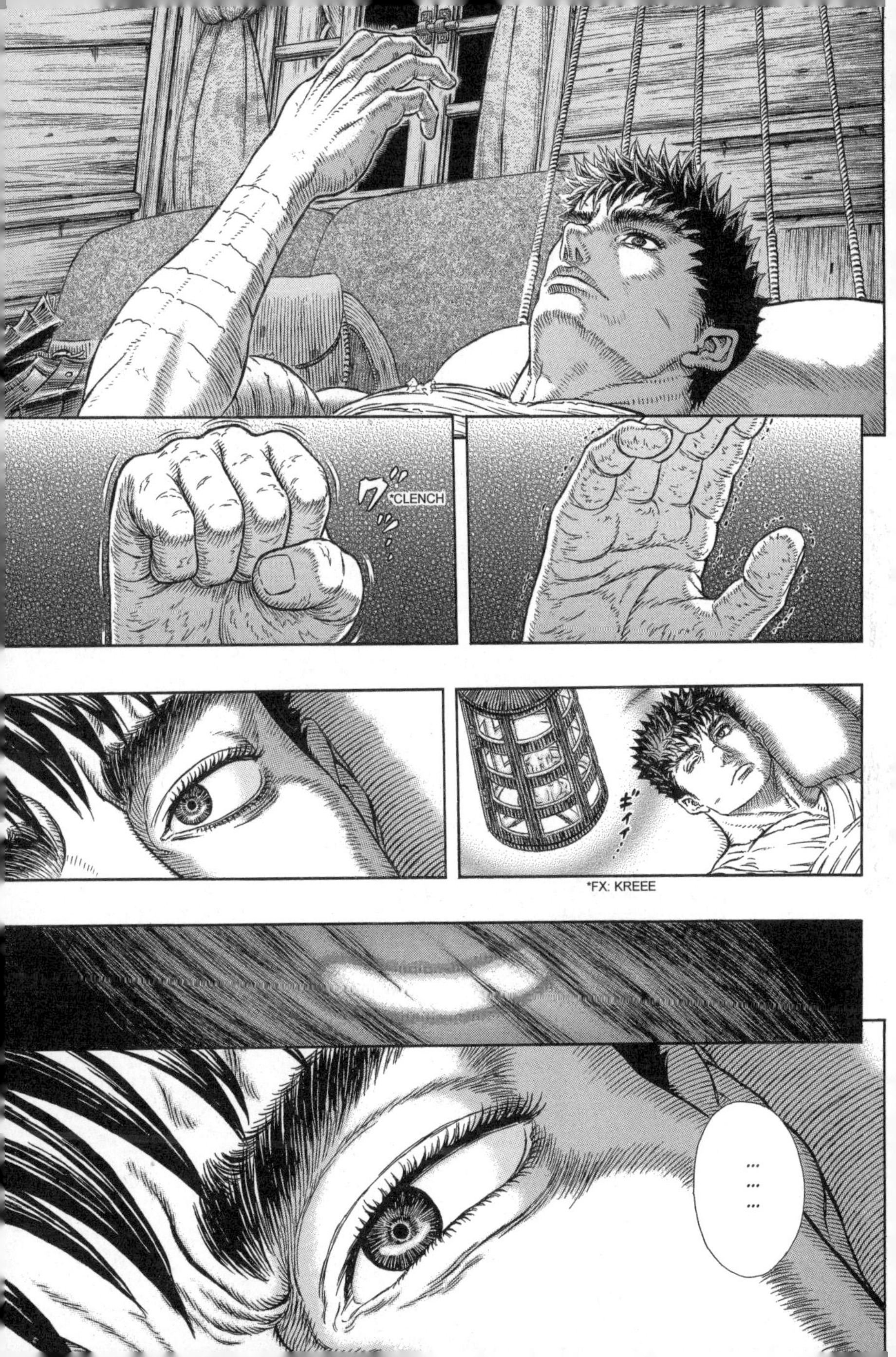
*CLENCH
*FX: KREEE
...
...
...

IT'S AN OMEN.
EACH TIME YOU WEAR THAT ARMOR AND FIGHT AS THE BERSERKER...
LIGHT...
VOICE...
WARMTH...
YOU WILL COME TO LOSE MANY THINGS.
THE OD THAT DWELLS IN THAT ARMOR IS AS A FLAME WHICH NEVER DIES OUT. EVEN ONCE CONTAINED, THE COALS YET SMOLDER. GIVEN THE CHANCE, IT WILL EXPLODE INTO HELLFIRE.
EVEN WITH AN APPLIED TALISMAN...
...NEVER MAKE LIGHT OF IT.
IF YOU...
...WISH TO CONTINUE EXISTING AS A HUMAN, THAT IS.
HE SAID IT LIKE IT'S PROPHECY, BUT THERE'S NO GUARANTEE IT'LL COME TRUE.
THIS VOYAGE IS PRACTICALLY ALMOST OVER. I JUST HAVE TO HOLD UP UNTIL THEN...
....
*KREEE
THE JOURNEY...
WILL BE OVER...

THERE'S NO GUARANTEE...
...YOUR WISH WILL BE HER WISH.
*BATHUMP
*BOLT
*KREEE
*KREEE
*HAHHH
*HAHHH

*HAH!
*HAH!
WHAT WILL SHE DO IF SHE DOES GET HER SANITY BACK...?
...THAT'S RIGHT, SHE WENT TO PIECES BECAUSE SHE CAN'T FULLY COPE WITH IT.
...
...
...
WHEN THIS JOURNEY ENDS...
I'LL...

WHAT IN THE HELL? IT LOOKS LIKE THERE'RE...
... BRANCHES ACROSS THE MOON.

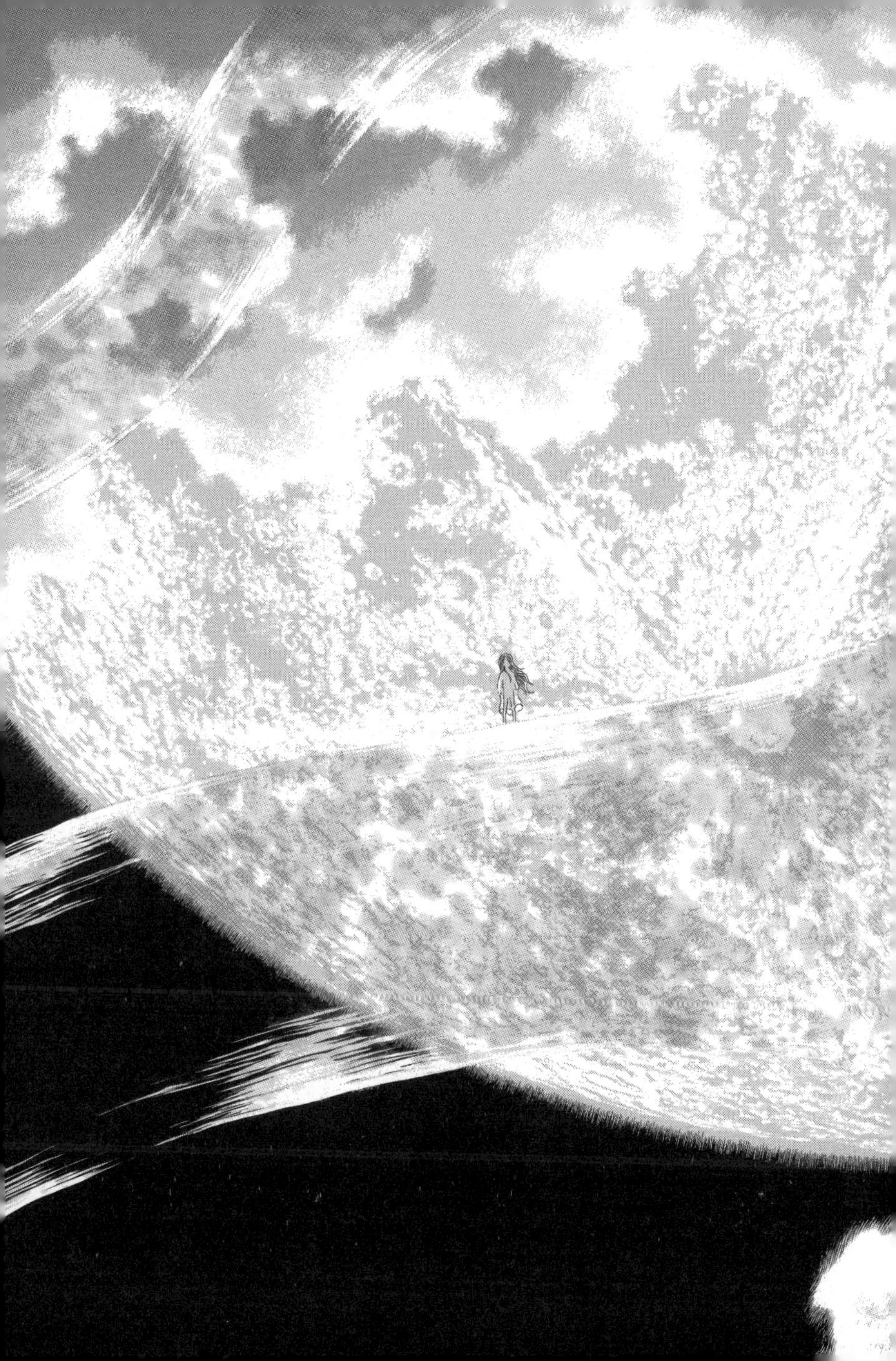

B E S E R K

遠い日の春花①

SPRING FLOWERS OF DISTANT DAYS, PART 1

I DON'T CARE WHERE I DROP DEAD.
THAT'S HOW THINGS SEEMED TO ME.
...IN THIS SHITTY WORLD OF THE BATTLEFIELD.
THAT LIFE DIDN'T EVEN MEAN ANYTHING...
*WHAPAA
GET UP, YOU!!
*FX: HAHH HAHH
*VYNN
*FX: THNK
WHY IS IT?

WHEN I GET KNOCKED DOWN...
...MY LEGS HAVE TO GO AND STAND BACK UP.

...
...
KEEP YOUR FOOTING, IF YOU WANT TO SURVIVE.
LOOKS LIKE WE HAVE A LONG WAY TO GO.
SHUT UP...
YOU OKAY, SONNY?
IT MUST BE GOD'S WILL.
UNLIKE NOBLES, WE MERCENARIES HAVE NO ONE TO PAY OUR RANSOM.
WE'RE LUCKY TO STILL BE ALIVE AFTER LOSING A BATTLE.
BESIDES, ALL MERCENARIES HACK PEOPLE UP FOR A LIVING.
WHY WOULD GOD CARE ABOUT PEOPLE LIKE US...?
*SWAY
HAHA... YOU'RE SLY, FOR A YOUNG'UN.
WON'T THEY JUST WORK US TO DEATH IN A MINE OR SOME-PLACE?
JUST MEANS WE'LL SUFFER LONGER.
STAY UPRIGHT, SONNY!
WHOA!

*YANK
DON'T YOU...
...EVER TOUCH ME...!!!
OKAY, OKAY.
NO NEED TO GLARE LIKE THAT.
YOU SERI-OUSLY DO LOOK PALE, THOUGH.
LEAVE OFF!
!
IS THAT AN ARROW WOUND?
UH-OH, YOU'RE BLEED-ING...!
SHUT UP!
MIND YOUR OWN--

*WHUNK
HEY...!
AW COME ON, AGAIN?
DON'T BE SUCH A BULLY.
HE'S JUST A KID.
*VSSHT
ARGH!
*HYNN
QUIT MAKING THIS HARDER!

EVEN A BOY CAN BE MAN-POWER, RIGHT?
IT'S YOUR LOSS IF HE DIES BEFORE YOU CAN PUT HIM TO WORK.
WHO CARES?! ANYONE WHO DIES GETS LEFT BEHIND!
WELL, HELL... THE RANK AND FILE SURE ARE STUBBORN.
GUESS I'LL HAVE TO HELP YOU.
COME ON, SONNY. STAND UP.
H-HEY...!
WHAT'RE...
...YOU DOING?
QUIT ACTING TOUGH.
YOU DON'T WANNA DIE IN A PLACE LIKE THIS, DO YOU?
...
...
...

I'M NOT FOR SALE.
AHA HA HA
DULY NOTED!
HEY.
YEAH?
YOU BEEN DOING THE MERCENARY THING FOR LONG, SONNY?
...MORE OR LESS.
YOU WANDER FROM BATTLE TO BATTLE?
... YEAH.
...AND AT YOUR AGE, TOO.
SOUNDS LIKE YOU'VE GOT A HISTORY.
... ...
WHOOPS, SORRY! I FORGOT, IT'S NOT THE MERCENARY WAY...
...TO GO AROUND SNOOPING INTO EACH OTHER'S SHADY PASTS.

BUT YOU KNOW...
...YOU KILL, AND YOU DIE.
MAYBE IT'S BECAUSE OF THAT ROTTEN-ASS BATTLEFIELD...
...THAT SOMEDAY, SOME-WHERE...
...YOU MIGHT MEET SOME WAR BUDDIES...
...AND FOR HIM... FOR THEM, IT'D BE KIND OF WORTH IT TO PUT YOUR LIFE ON THE LINE.
'COURSE...
...THAT'S ASSUMING YOU LIVE LONG ENOUGH FOR IT TO HAPPEN.

HEY, LOOK. A CASTLE WAY BACK IN THE MOUNTAINS. THAT MUST BE OUR DESTINATION.
IT LOOKS LIKE THEY'RE STILL BUILDING IT...
AHA, AND WE'RE THE LABORERS WHO'LL CARRY THE STONES.
HEY, SONNY.
HERE
カチャ
*CLICK
WHA ...?
ONCE YOU'RE IN THAT CASTLE, GETTING OUT WOULD BE A BIT TRICKY.
NOW'S YOUR ONLY CHANCE TO ESCAPE.
RUN LIKE HELL DOWN THAT CLIFF. I DOUBT THEY'LL CATCH YOU, ON HORSEBACK OR WEARING ARMOR.
THEN LET'S TIME IT AND BOTH RUN.
I'M AFRAID I CAN'T.
I'LL NEVER UNLOCK MY OWN SHACKLES WITH THIS.
MY HAND WON'T REACH.
JUST GO WITHOUT ME.
HARD LABOR'S LIKE A DEATH SENTENCE IN YOUR SHAPE.
IF YOU WERE CRUSHED BY A STONE YOU WERE CARRYING, HEY, THAT'D BE YOUR TOMB-STONE.
BUT MERCENARIES DON'T GET LUXURIES LIKE THAT.
... ...

WHAT'S YOUR NAME?
MARTINO.
I'M GUTS.
*FX: DANGLE
I'LL PAY...
...YOU BACK SOMEDAY.
!
ONE GOT LOOSE!
*SHFFFFF
AFTER HIM!
DON'T LET HIM ESCAPE!!

*KRIK
*KRIK
...YOU'RE GOING TO PAY ME BACK RIGHT NOW...
*FX: TUG
ACTU-ALLY...
...SONNY.
*VYNN
*SHF
*SHF
*SHF
*VNN
DAMN IT...! MY INJURY...!
*THWAK
*THWING

*THNK
*THNK
*CHFF
*SHFFFF
IS HE DEAD?
WE MISSED ANYTHING VITAL.
GREAT, WAY TO SLOW US DOWN.
*YANK
C'MON!
ON YOUR FEET, BOY!

WE DON'T KNOW WHERE THE ENEMY'S LYING IN AMBUSH...
SO WE'LL JUST HAVE TO ALL RUSH THEM! FORTUNE FAVORS THE BOLD!!
BRACE YOURSELVES, NEW GUYS!
THE FIRST ONE TO CUT INTO THE ENEMY LINES WILL GET THREE SILVER COINS!
*ROHHHHH
EVERY-BODY CHARGE!!

*GRIN
*GRIN
*ZHAAAA
*THNK
*THNK
*THNK
*THNK
*THNK

OKAY! THE AMBUSH IS IN THAT THICKET!
FIRE AWAY!!
*WHOMP
*BOOOOM
HEY.
YOU'RE STILL ALIVE.
UNHH...
*ROHHHHH
GOOD JOB.
YOU MADE A GREAT DECOY.

ALL THE REST WHO CHARGED...
THEY'RE DEAD.
DEATH'S PART OF THE JOB FOR MERCENARIES.
GAMBINO...
WHAT'S WITH THE SULLEN FACE?
IT WAS GOOD EXPERIENCE, WASN'T IT? PLUS, YOU'RE STILL ALIVE. WHAT'S THERE TO SAY?
LISTEN, GUTS.
IF YOU WANT TO SURVIVE ON THE BATTLEFIELD...
...GET BY WITH YOUR OWN BRAINS AND SKILLS.
DON'T DEPEND ON OTHERS.
PEOPLE WILL DO DESPICABLE THINGS FOR THEIR OWN AMBITION, OR TO SURVIVE.
THAT'S WHAT IT BOILS DOWN TO ON THE BATTLEFIELD.
THOSE WHO BLINDLY FOLLOW OTHERS OUT HERE JUST GET CHEWED UP, SPAT OUT, AND KILLED.
WELL...
TAKE IT AS FATHERLY ADVICE.
DON'T EVEN TRUST YOUR FATHER OUT HERE.
...
C'MON.
IF YOU CAN STAND UP...
...GO EARN SOME MONEY.

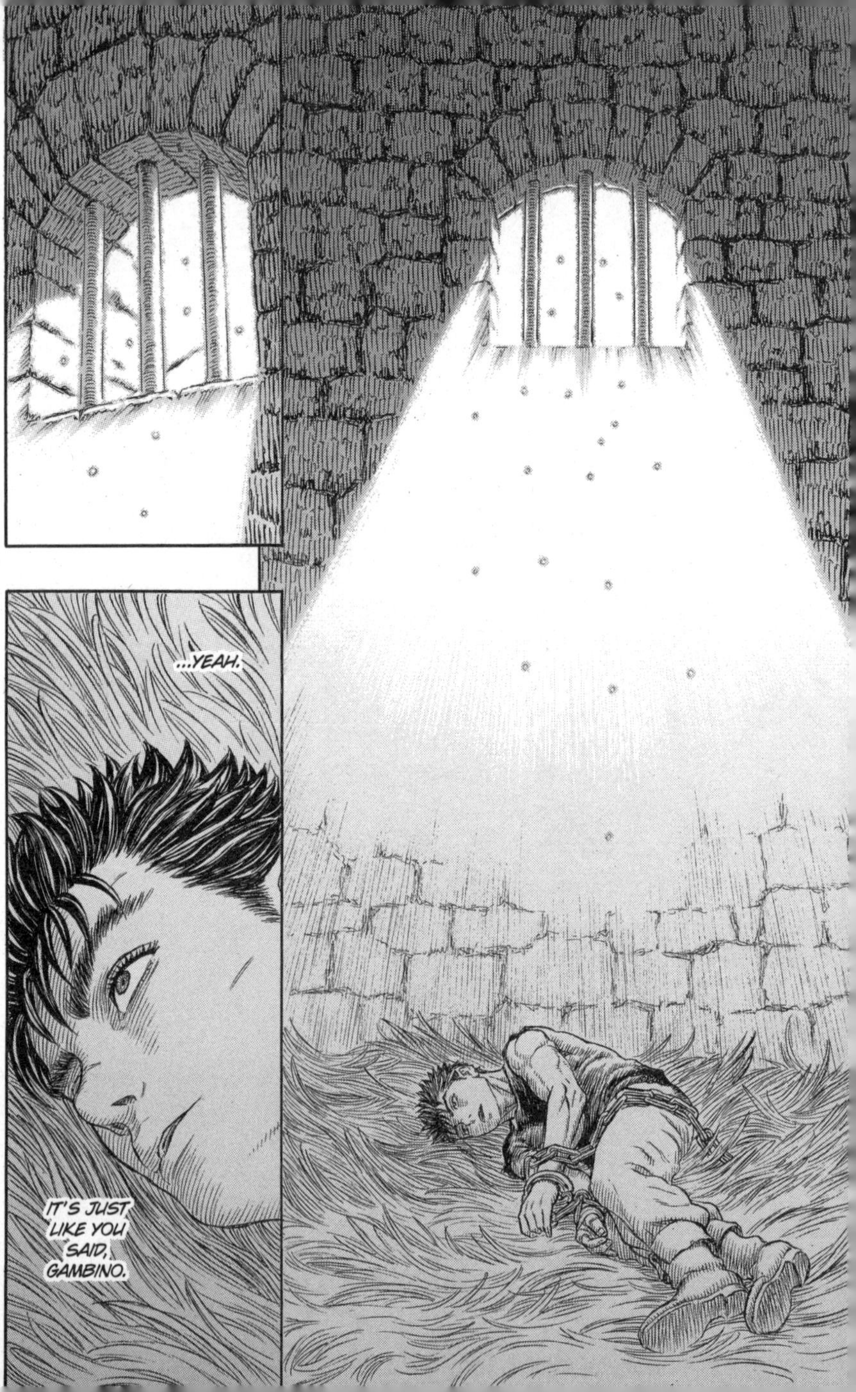
...YEAH.
IT'S JUST LIKE YOU SAID, GAMBINO.

SOMEDAY...
SOMEWHERE.
DID I LET MY GUARD DOWN OVER A CLICHÉ?
THAT MAKES ME A LAUGHINGSTOCK.
I FEEL WEAK.
I'M COLD...
I LOST TOO MUCH BLOOD.
....
SOMEDAY, SOMEWHERE.
THOSE WORDS DON'T BELONG ANYWHERE NEAR A BATTLEFIELD.

I DON'T CARE WHEN OR WHERE I DROP DEAD.
EVEN NOW...
...I DON'T.
チ チ...
*FX: CHITCH CHITCH
*SNATCH
*CHOMP
*RRRRIP

WHY...?
*FX: GUSH
WHY'D...
...I DO IT AGAIN...?
*FX: SHFF
......
A SINGLE FLOWER...
...IN THIS COLD GODDAMN CELL ...
GUESS THAT MAKES US CELLMATES...

なずな
薺

遠い日の春花②

SPRING FLOWERS OF DISTANT DAYS, PART 2

WHAT...?
IS THIS...
...SOME KIND OF FEVER DREAM?
*GCHAK
*KREEE
ガチャ
ギイイ
*LOOM
ヌッ
STAND HIM UP.
*FX: GSHANG GSHANG
ガシャ
ガシャ
HE'S OF A SUIT-ABLE AGE.

BOY...
HOW ARE YOUR INJURIES?
*FX: PTOO
*FX: PLAP
BAS-TARD!
*WHACK
*WHUNK
HOW DARE YOU ACT THAT WAY TOWARD THE VISCOUNT...?!
YOU'VE HIT HIM ENOUGH.
BUT, MILORD ...
NOW I KNOW FOR SURE HE'S *LIVELY.*
MORE IMPORTANTLY, I CAN'T HAVE YOU TORMENT HIM SO MUCH HE BECOMES *UNUSABLE.*
THAT WON'T DO.
!
HEY, BRING MEDICINE.
YES, MI-LORD ...!
YOU NEEDN'T DO THIS PERSONALLY, MILORD...
NO MATTER.
... ...

WHAT'S THE BIG IDEA? THIS'S SICK.
YOU HAVE ALL THESE ARROW WOUNDS, YET LISTEN TO YOU GO.
HMHM... YOU'RE MOST PROMIS-ING.
THERE, THAT SHOULD DO.
カチャ
*CHAK
YOU SEE, YOU'RE GOING TO DO A JOB FOR ME TOMORROW.
YOU'RE GOING TO...
...OFFER YOUR LIFE...
...FOR MY SON'S SAKE.
HE'S SOON GOING TO FIGHT HIS FIRST BATTLE.
HE'S A FINE BOY, BUT HE CAN BE A BIT TOO TENDER-HEARTED.

I WANT TO BOLSTER HIS NERVE A BIT BEFORE HE GOES OFF TO WAR.
THAT'S WHY YOU AND HE WILL FIGHT TO THE DEATH. CONVENIENTLY, *HE'LL* KILL *YOU.*
YOU THINK SO?
I GET THAT A LOT.
ISN'T THAT DOTING DADDY...?
...DO-TARD DADDY.
Y-YOU *LOUT!*
WELL, WE CAN'T FEED YOU, AS WE CAN'T HAVE YOU *TOO* ENER-GETIC...
BUT TAKE CARE OF YOURSELF, BOY.
... ...
*BTAM

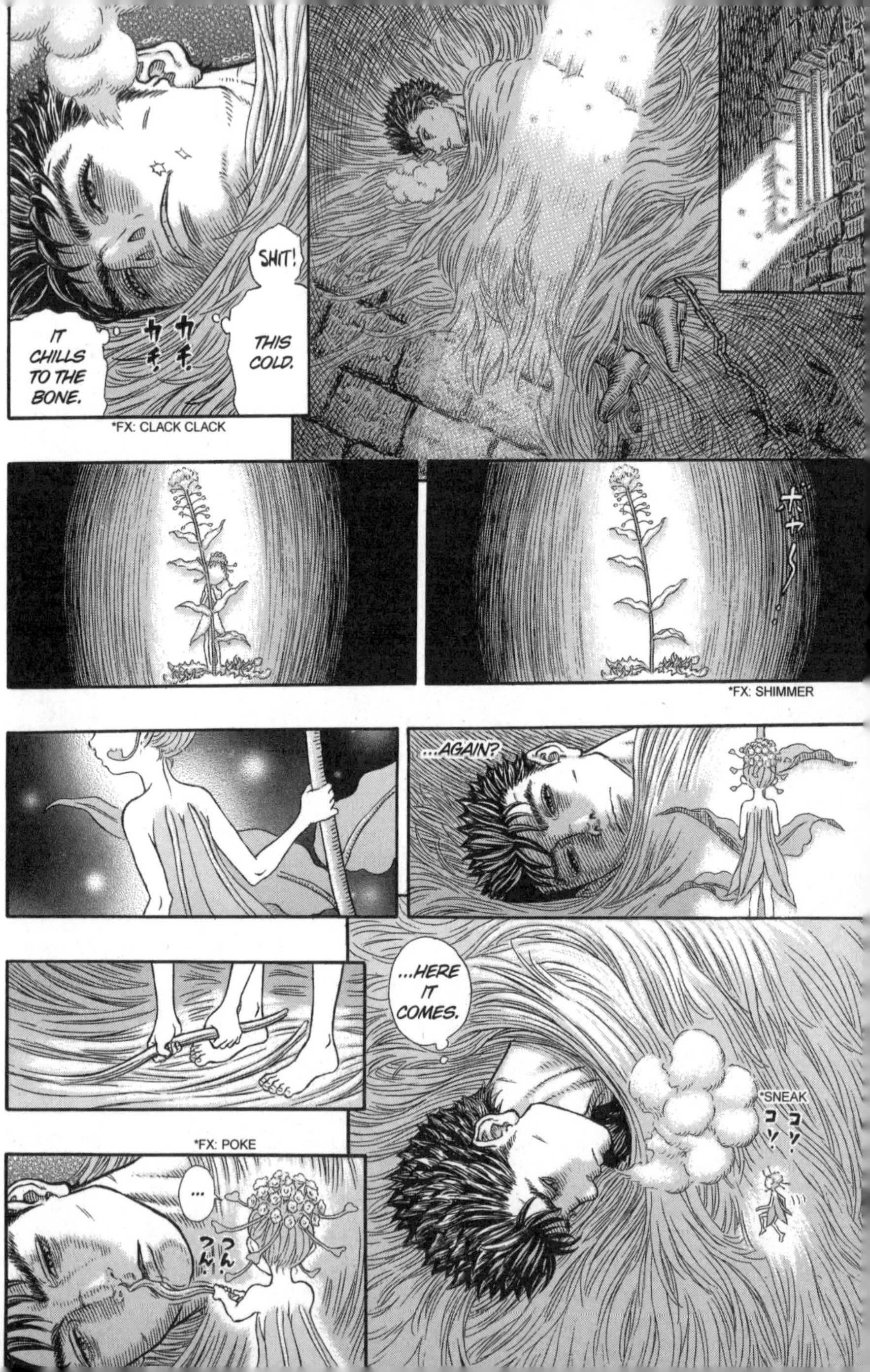
SHIT!
THIS COLD.
カチ カチ
IT CHILLS TO THE BONE.
*FX: CLACK CLACK
ボヤ～
*FX: SHIMMER
...AGAIN?
...HERE IT COMES.
コソ コソ
*SNEAK
*FX: POKE
...
つん つん

*ACHOO
*FX: SHOOM
*FX: SCOOT
NO NEED TO BE SO JUMPY.
GREAT... I'M TALKING TO A HALLUCINATION.
*FX: SNFF
HEY ...
...
IS THAT YOUR FLOWER?
RELAX, I'M NOT GONNA PLUCK IT.
WE'RE BOTH STUCK IN THIS CELL.
MIGHT AS WELL GET ALONG.
WON'T PLUCK ...
GET ALONG.
GET ALONG ...
...WITH HUMAN?
*TRUDGE
HI.
WELL, THIS'LL KILL TIME.

CHITCH IS CHITCH.
SPIRIT OF THE FLOWER.
RAT SAID "CHITCH," SO AM *CHITCH.*
I'M GUTS.
NICE TO MEET YOU, HALLUCINATION.
NOT HALLUCINATION.
CHITCH IS CHITCH ...
GUTS HUMAN.
WAS SAVED BY GUTS HUMAN. RAT WAS EATING.
LITTLE LONGER AND *ALL* CHITCH'S LEAVES EATEN.
THEN, CHITCH DISAPPEAR.
ASK FOR ANYTHING AS THANKS.
OH, YEAH ?
...THEN COULD YOU OPEN THE DOOR TO THIS CELL, AND STEAL THE KEY ...?
CAN'T.
CAN'T YOU...?
CHITCH FLOWER SPIRIT, SO CAN'T GO TOO FAR FROM FLOWER.
SHE'S PRETTY STUBBORN, FOR A DREAM.

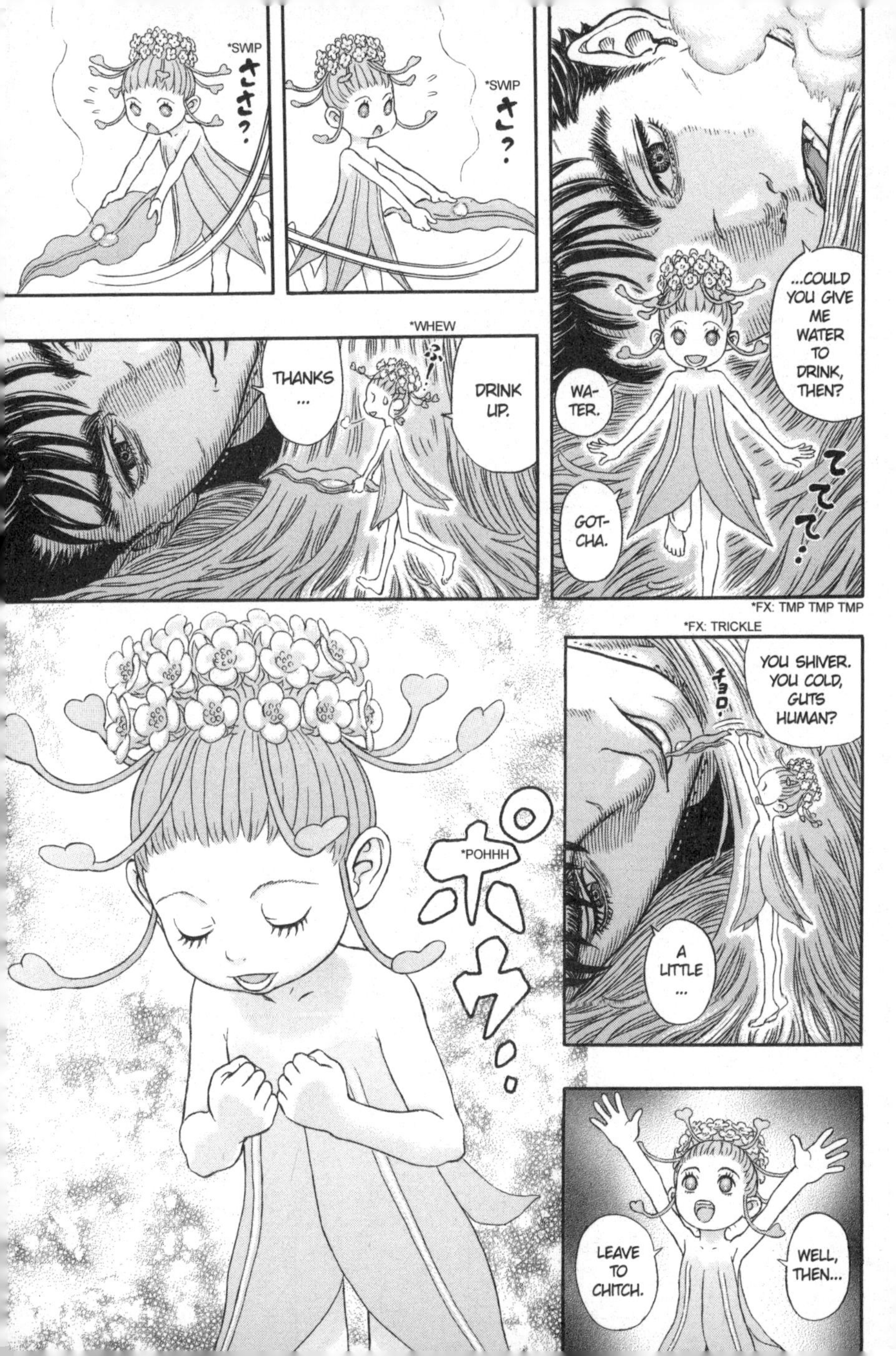

...COULD YOU GIVE ME WATER TO DRINK, THEN?
WA-TER.
GOT-CHA.
ててて..
*FX: TMP TMP TMP
さっ
*SWIP
ささっ
*SWIP
DRINK UP.
ふ
*WHEW
THANKS ...
*FX: TRICKLE
チョロ
YOU SHIVER. YOU COLD, GUTS HUMAN?
A LITTLE ...
WELL, THEN...
LEAVE TO CHITCH.
ポウ
*POHHH

...THAT'S WARM.
...
...
I STOPPED SHIVERING...
IS WARM, HUH? CHITCH'S BODY FILLED WITH WARM POPPO FROM SUN.
WELL? WELL?
MORE?
POPO-POPOHH
*SPIN
*SPIN
LOOKS LIKE FUN.
MMM, IS FUN. POPPO FUN BY ITSELF...
BUT POPPO WITH SOMEONE ELSE MORE POPOPOPOHH. SO STRANGE!

*CRAWL
*CRAWL
HEY! QUIT CLIMBIN' ON ME!
YOU'RE GETTIN' A LITTLE TOO FRIENDLY...
GUTS HUMAN BLEEDING.
THAT STUPID NOBLE DIDN'T EXACTLY PATCH ME UP RIGHT...
...!
?
WHAT WRONG?
LOOKS REALLY PAIN-FUL!
LOOKS PAIN-FUL!
NO, IT'S NO BIG DEAL...
HNNN...
*SNPT
... WHAT'RE YOU DOIN'?
LEAVE TO CHITCH.
*FWEP
*SSSSS
......

THE PAIN'S GONE.
THANKS. I FEEL A LOT BETTER.
くる くる くる
*FX: SPIN SPIN SPIN
YEAH? EHEEHEE!
IS LIKE, SO POPO-POPOHH.
AMAZING, HUH?
BIRD ONCE GOT HURT AND FELL IN HERE. CHITCH HEALED IT WITH POWER OF LEAVES.
プチ
*FX: SNPT
DO MY OTHER INJURIES, IF YOU CAN.
CHITCH WILL, WILL.
NOW I SHOULD BE ABLE TO MOVE.
ピタ
*STOP
?
WHAT'S WRONG?
......
WILL LEAVE?
ONCE CAN MOVE AGAIN...
...GUTS HUMAN...
...WILL LEAVE, TOO?

SOME-TIMES HUMANS COME HERE...
BUT ALL JUST MOAN AND YELL...
CHITCH WAS KINDA SCARED.
THEN THEY SOON LEAVE.
......
THERE NOTHING IN HERE.
POPPO COME THROUGH THAT HOLE, THEN GET DARK, THEN POPPO, THEN DARK AGAIN...
THAT ALL.
BECAUSE WHEN POPPO COME...
...QUIET, DARK SHINSHIN COME LATER.
CHITCH LIKE POPPO...
BUT ALSO NOT LIKE.
JUST CHITCH.

……
……
……
THIS HALLUCINATION OF MINE...
...IS REALLY MY WEAKNESS, IN THE FORM OF A KID...
*FX: SHFF
ガサ
コロ…
*ROLL
ぽて
*WHMP
?
……
……
……

PWEE ?
ギュ
*SQUEEZE
ON THE WAY TO THIS CASTLE...
?
?
...I HAPPENED TO SEE A HILL WHERE FLOWERS LIKE YOURS... WHERE A BUNCH OF YOUR BUDDIES WERE BLOOMING.
ONCE I CAN MOVE AGAIN...
...I'LL TAKE YOU AND YOUR FLOWER THERE.

REALLY? REALLY? GUTS HUMAN!
SURE.
REALLY REALLY REALLY?
SURE.
ちょろ
ちょろ
ちょろ
*FX: DART DART DART
*GLOMP みよん.
REALLY REALLY REALLY REALLY REA--?
I PRO-MISE.
POPPO!
FEEL Soooo PoPPo NOW!
HEAL!
CHITCH HEAL ALL GUTS HUMAN'S WOUNDS!
MAKE YOU MOVE MORE THAN RAT DID!
IS IT OKAY TO TEAR OFF THAT MANY?
*SNPT
*SNPT
LEAVE TO CHITCH. GUTS HUMAN SLEEP, SLEEP.
*FWUP
OKAY, OKAY. DO YOUR THING, THEN.
MMMM
CAN'T HELP BUT POPPO.
GUTS HUMAN ONLY ONE...

GUTS HUMAN ONLY ONE...
...TO FIND CHITCH.
OH, YEAH ...?
BUDDIES.
WILL FIND CHITCH?
WONDER IF THEY WILL.
*FX: FWAHHH
WELL, IF WE GO TO THAT HILL...
...YOUR BUDDIES WILL PROBABLY ALL FIND YOU.
THEY'LL FIND YOU.
BET ON IT...
THE WARMTH ON MY BACK THAT WAS LIKE A LITTLE SUNNY SPOT...
...WAS STILL THERE EVEN AFTER I FELL ASLEEP.

MY FEVER BROKE.
DID I SLEEP A WHOLE DAY AND NIGHT...?
...NO WAY.
HEY...
AND MY WOUNDS...
*FX: DROP
... ...
HEY... CHITCH.
YOU'RE KIDDING ME.

IT WASN'T...
...A DREAM?
I WASN'T DREAMING...
...THAT MY WORTHLESS SOFT-HEART-EDNESS...
...TOOK THE FORM OF A KID...
...AND SHOWED UP TO BUG ME...?

...
...
...
YOU IDIOT...
THAT'S THE PROBLEM WITH KIDS...
DID YOU GET SO CAUGHT UP IN THE MOMENT...
...YOU DIDN'T THINK ABOUT THE CONSE-QUENCES...
...AND YOU PLUCKED **ALL** YOUR LEAVES?
HEY, CHITCH!
ARE YOU HERE ?!
COME ON OUT!!
HEY...!
...
...
...
THE VISCOUNT WANTS YOU!
*FX: CHAK CHAK

……
OUT!
BTAM

なずな
薺

遠い日の春花③

SPRING FLOWERS OF DISTANT DAYS, PART 3

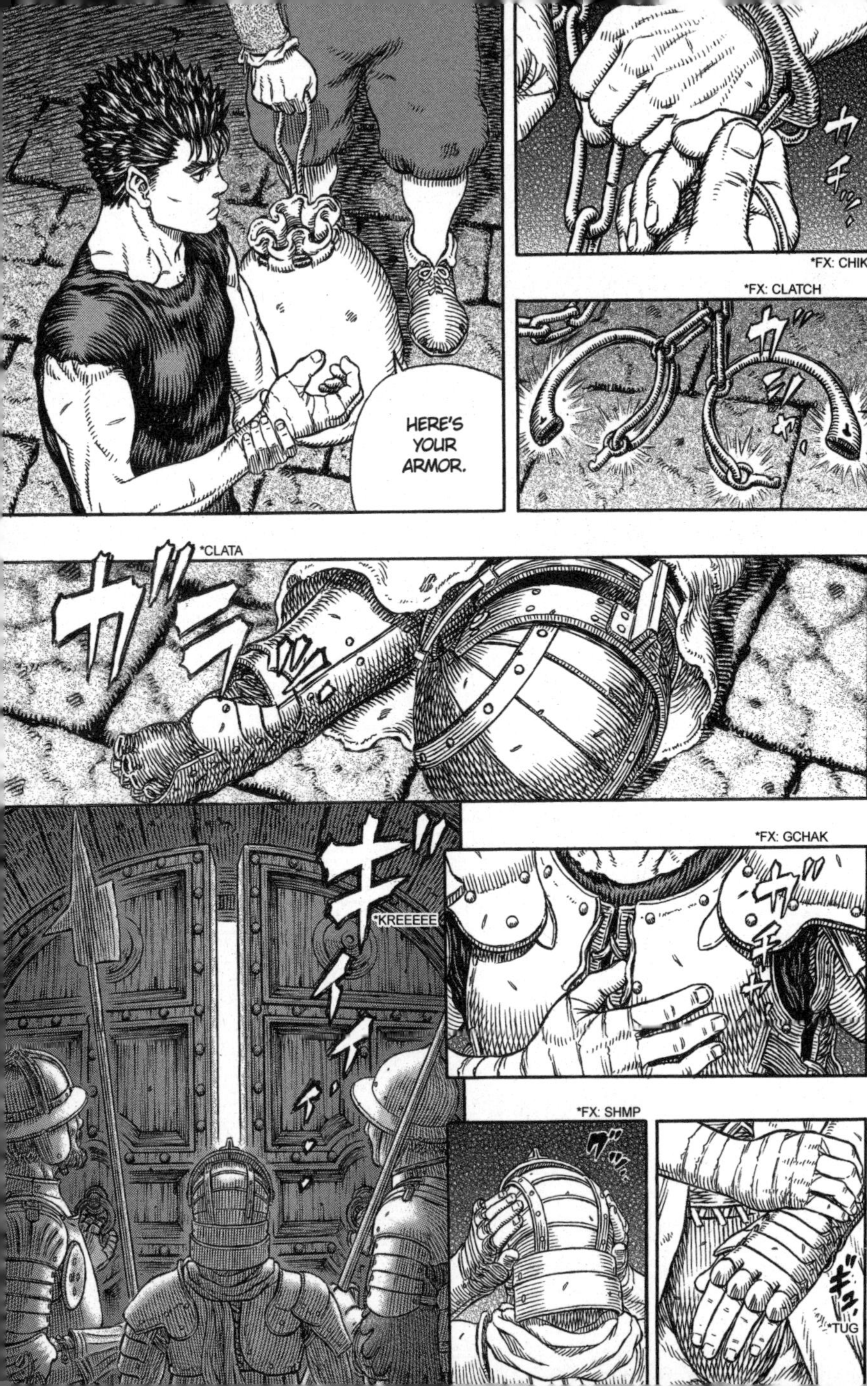
*FX: CHIK
*FX: CLATCH
HERE'S YOUR ARMOR.
*CLATA
*FX: GCHAK
*TUG
*FX: SHMP
*KREEEEE

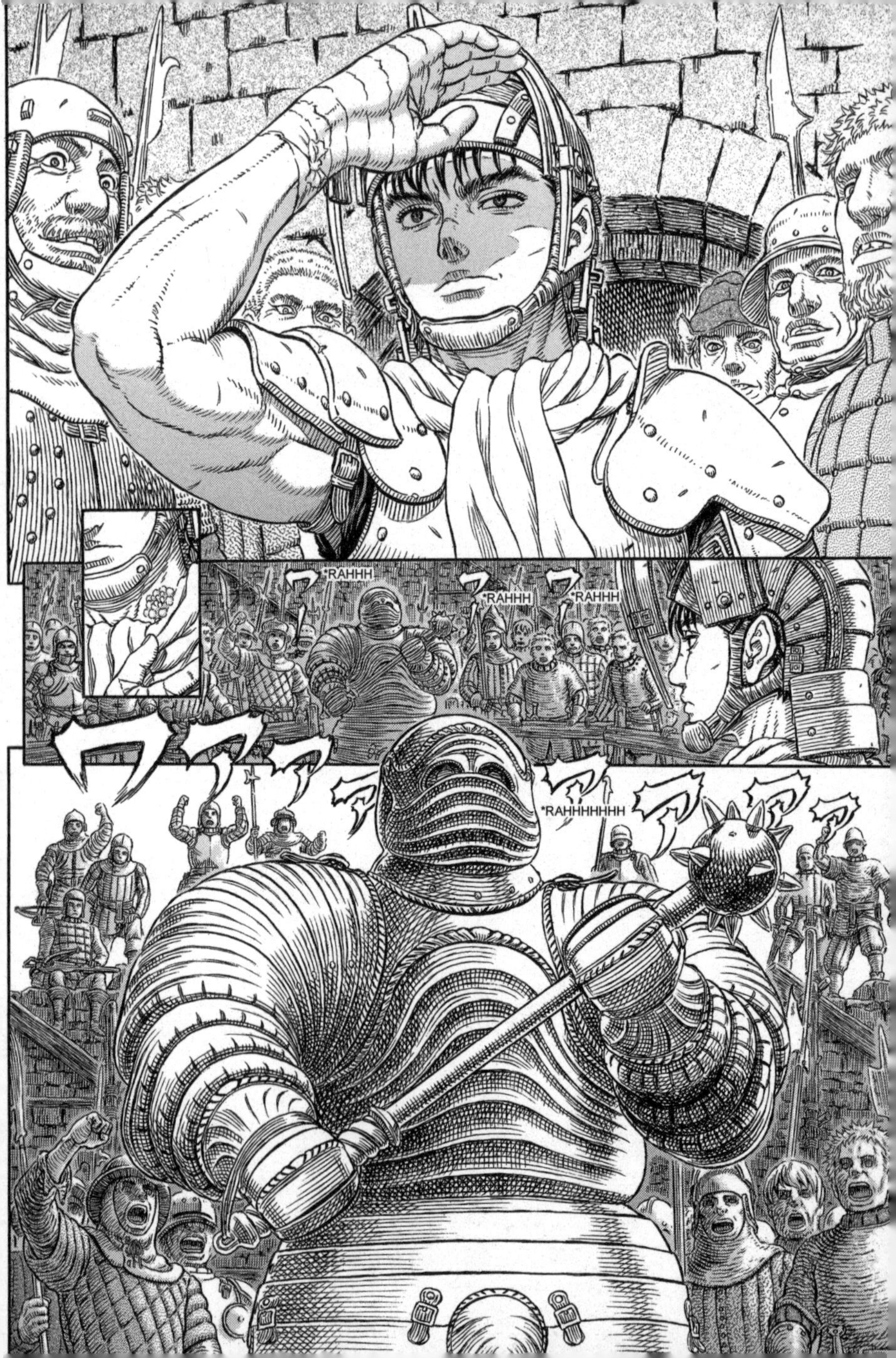
*RAHHH
*RAHHH
*RAHHH
*RAHHHHHHH

SLAYING A MAN IS THE SAME AS HUNTING.
JUST DEAL WITH HIM AS YOU WOULD SOME WILD BOAR.
NOW, THERE'S NO NEED TO GET TOO WORKED UP.
FIGHT WELL, SON!
... ...
WE NEEDN'T WORRY, IF YOU CAN MANAGE THAT RETORT.
IF I CAN'T, CAN I GO BACK TO SLEEP?
CAN YOU MOVE AROUND, BOY?
BUT WHEN HE TRIED TO ABDUCT AND BEHEAD A LOCAL PEASANT CHILD, THE VISCOUNT ADMONISHED HIM FOR IT, AND SO, HERE WE ARE TODAY.
LIKE DOTARD DADDY, LIKE STUPID SON.
BRAHHHHH
VNN
VNN
AS YOU CAN SEE, THE YOUNG MASTER HAS A BIT OF A VIOLENT TEMPER. HE'S ENJOYED BLOODSHED SINCE HE WAS A BOY, AND WOULD BEHEAD LIVESTOCK AND THE LIKE DURING HIS PLAY.
THE BLADE'S IN POOR SHAPE, SO YOU KNOW.
YOU'D HAVE A HARD TIME CUTTING WATERMELON, WITH THIS.
WELL, STRUGGLE AS BEST YOU CAN.
HERE.

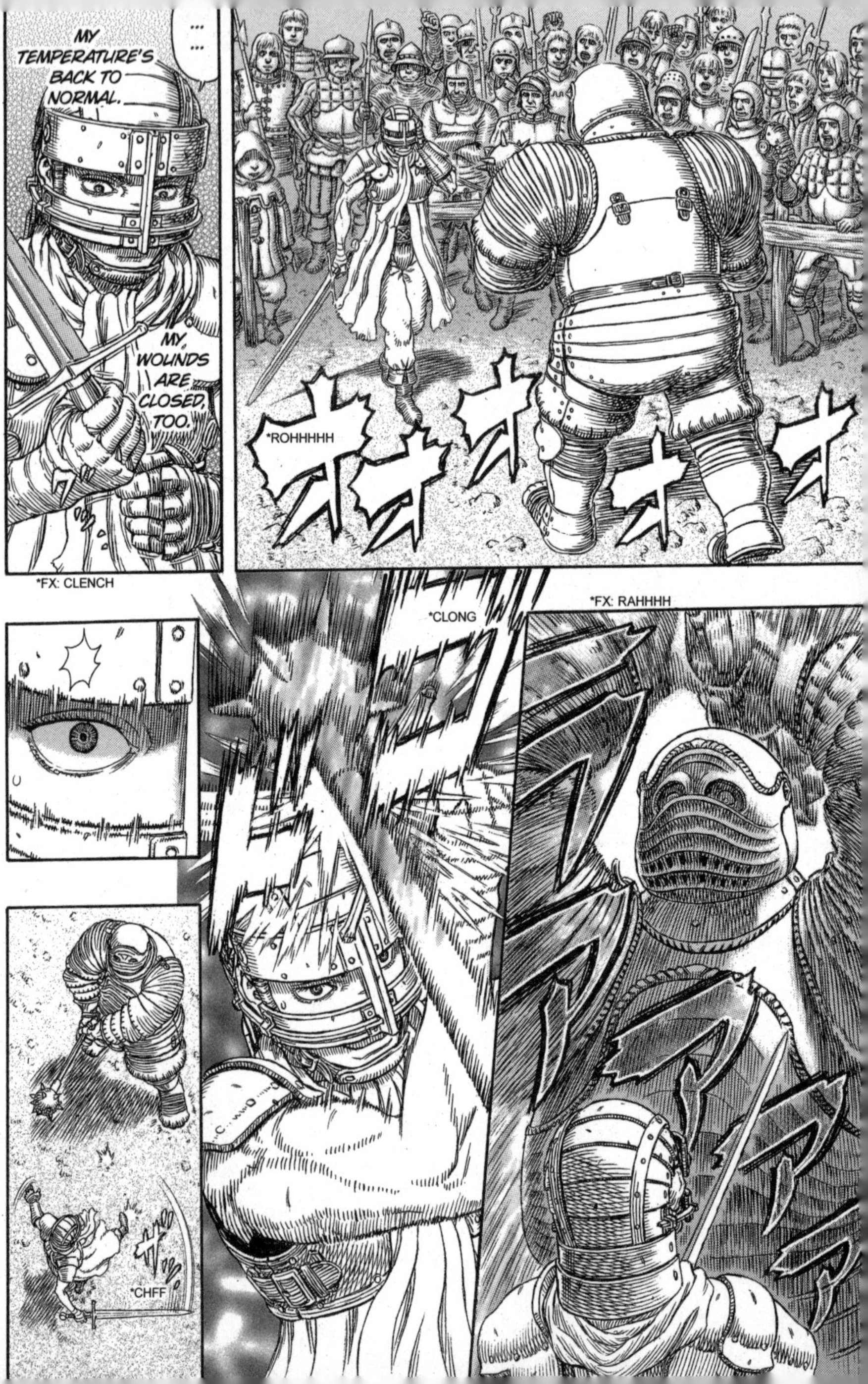
*ROHHHHH
... ...
MY TEMPERATURE'S BACK TO NORMAL.
MY WOUNDS ARE CLOSED, TOO.
*FX: CLENCH
*FX: RAHHHH
*CLONG
*CHFF

I DON'T HAVE ANY STRENGTH...!!
*ORAHHH
*WHOM
*JINNNG
*GLONG
*SHOM
*VNNN
*GAJING

*CLANG
*WHOCK
*CHFFF
*URAHHHH
SEE THAT? SEE THAT?! HE SENT HIM FLYING! IT'S AS GOOD AS OVER!
BRAVO, MILORD.
IT JUST MIGHT BE THAT MY SON...
...HAS THE POTENTIAL TO BE A GREAT GENERAL.
MOST INSIGHTFUL, MILORD.
*ROHHH

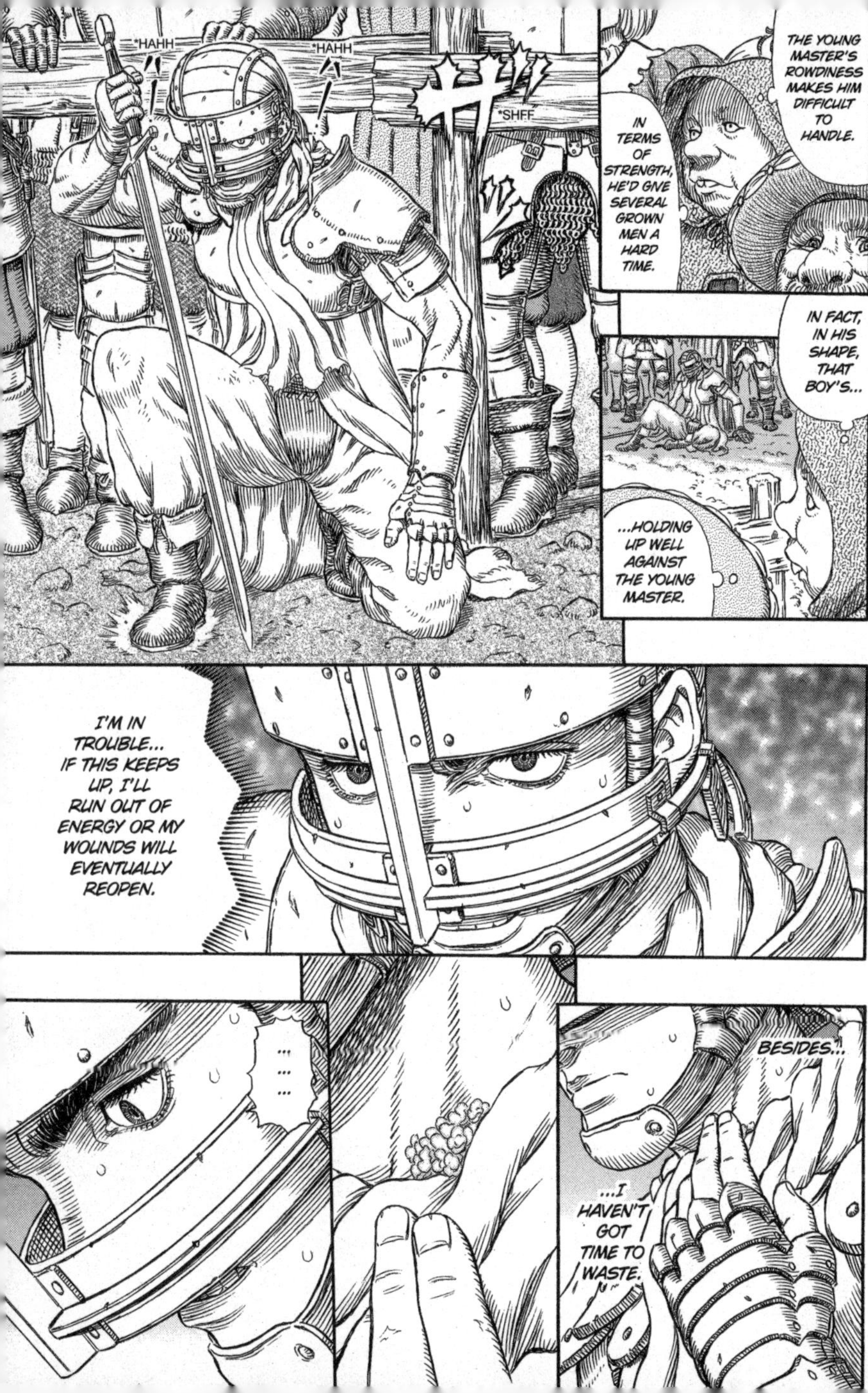
THE YOUNG MASTER'S ROWDINESS MAKES HIM DIFFICULT TO HANDLE.
IN TERMS OF STRENGTH, HE'D GIVE SEVERAL GROWN MEN A HARD TIME.
*HAHH
*HAHH
*SHFF
IN FACT, IN HIS SHAPE, THAT BOY'S...
...HOLDING UP WELL AGAINST THE YOUNG MASTER.
I'M IN TROUBLE... IF THIS KEEPS UP, I'LL RUN OUT OF ENERGY OR MY WOUNDS WILL EVENTUALLY REOPEN.
BESIDES...
...I HAVEN'T GOT TIME TO WASTE.
...
...
...

*OHHHH
*YANK
*CLANG
*SHFF
HNNN...
*KRRRN
*CLONNNG
*FX: KRUNK

*KRAK
...OKAY THEN!
*VWOM
*CHINNNG
*CHFFF
THAT WON'T GET THROUGH EITHER ...!
*SHUFF
*VWOM
*GRAHHHH!
WHAT A SCARE! THAT BOY'S GOOD.
*WHEW
BUT MY SON'S ARMOR IS CHUDER-MADE IMPREGNABLE FULL MAIL.
THERE'S NO GAP A BLADE CAN GET THROUGH, EVEN AT THE JOINTS!

USUALLY, MY FIRST BLOW SHOULD HAVE BROKEN OPEN BOTH HIS HELMET AND HEAD...
BUT I DON'T EVEN HAVE HALF MY USUAL STRENGTH. MY SWORD'S BLUNT, TOO, AND THE TIP JUST CHIPPED OFF.
*FX: GRAHHHH
NOW...
WHAT DO I DO?
*ROHHHHH
GAM-BINO!
*CLONG
*CLANG
*CHING

REMEMBER THIS WELL, GUTS.
THAT'S THICK, AND THERE'S NO GAP FOR A BLADE TO GET THROUGH.
IT'S A SAFE BET THAT ANYONE DRESSED IN ARMOR LIKE THIS IS A RICH NOBLE.
IN THAT CASE...
...THERE'S ONLY ONE WAY FOR US TO EARN OUR PAY ON THE BATTLEFIELD.
*WHAM
*CLANNNG
*WHOM
*CHUK

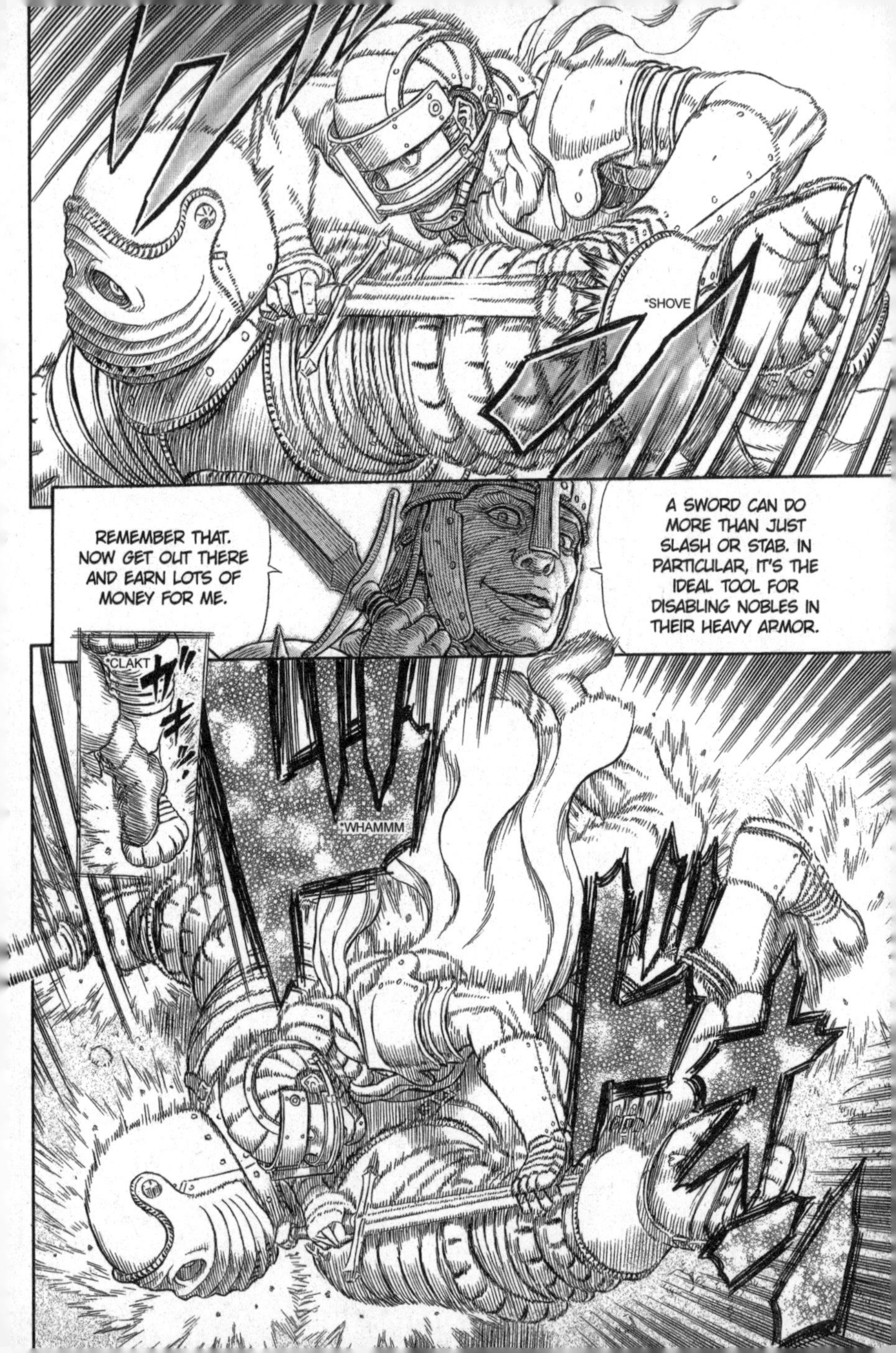
*SHOVE
A SWORD CAN DO MORE THAN JUST SLASH OR STAB. IN PARTICULAR, IT'S THE IDEAL TOOL FOR DISABLING NOBLES IN THEIR HEAVY ARMOR.
REMEMBER THAT. NOW GET OUT THERE AND EARN LOTS OF MONEY FOR ME.
*CLAKT
*WHAMMM

*GRIND
*GRIND
HNGGH... MY ARRRM...!!
*CHOLK
*HYNN
*AUGHHHHH
S-SONNNN!

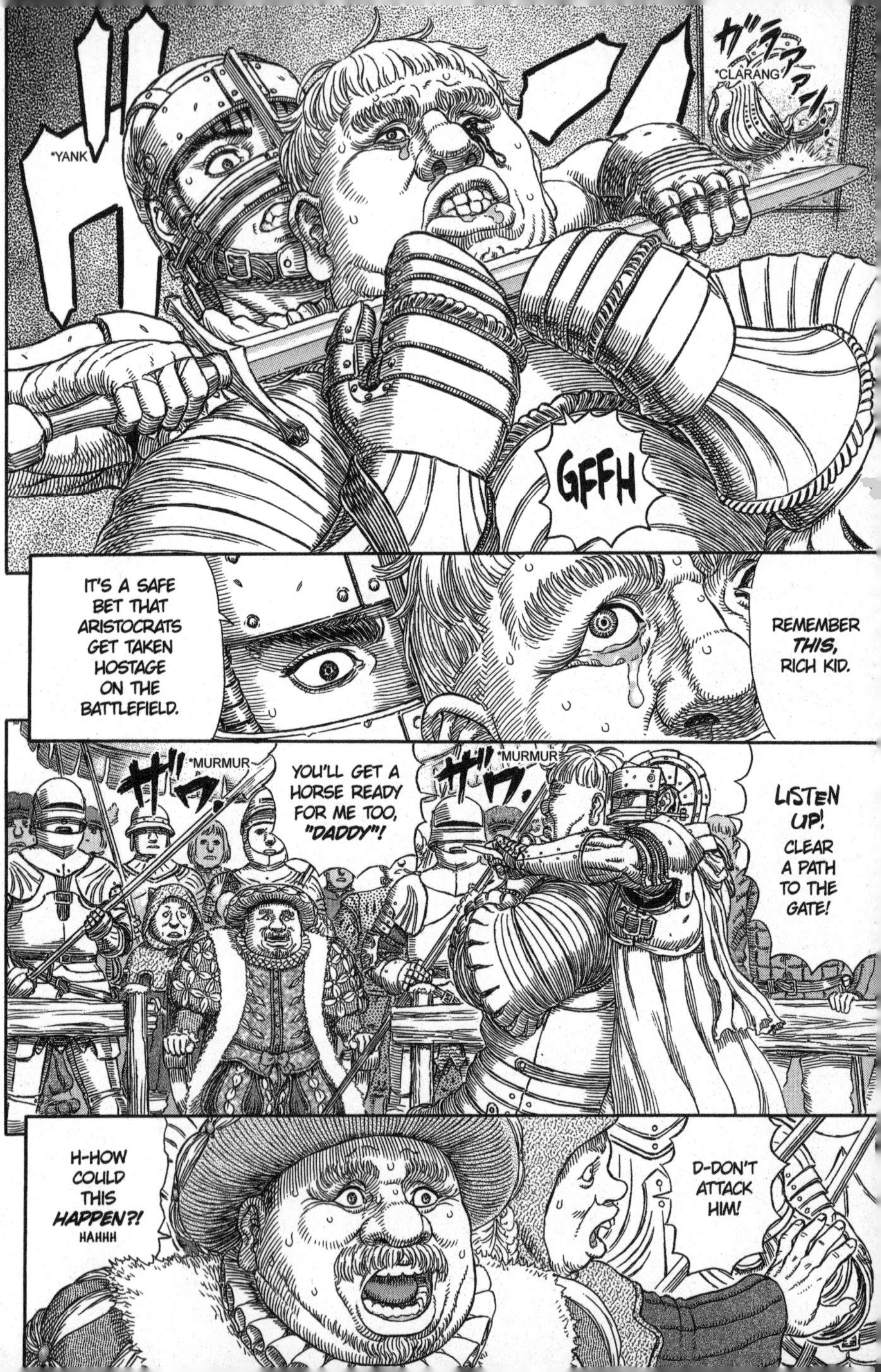

*CLARANG
*YANK
GFFH
REMEMBER THIS, RICH KID.
IT'S A SAFE BET THAT ARISTOCRATS GET TAKEN HOSTAGE ON THE BATTLEFIELD.
LISTEN UP! CLEAR A PATH TO THE GATE!
*MURMUR
YOU'LL GET A HORSE READY FOR ME TOO, "DADDY"!
*MURMUR
D-DON'T ATTACK HIM!
H-HOW COULD THIS HAPPEN?!
HAHHH

F--
FAWDDER
...
I CAN HARDLY EVEN HOLD MY SWORD ANYMORE. CAN I GET THROUGH THIS?
*INCH
*INCH
NOT YET. YOU'LL HIT THE YOUNG MASTER. WAIT FOR HIM TO TURN HIS BACK...
*WHSSSSS

*THNK
S-STUPID, WHY'D YOU ...?!
AW, NO...!
Y-YOUNG MASTER!
*THUD
MILORD ...!
HNNN...
*YEEEEEE
*HYN
*HYN
*THNK
*THNK
*THNK

?!
*AUGHHHH
WHAT'S GOING ON?!
*RMMMBLE
ATTACK...! WE'RE UNDER ATTACK!!
!
ガラ
*CLATA
ガラ
*CLATA
ガラ
*CLATA
ガラ
*CLATA

DMDMDMDMDM

*RMMMBLE

*CLOP
*CLOP
*CLOP
HO THERE, BOY! YOU'RE STILL ALIVE?!
*CLOP
...IT'S YOU?
*YEEEE
YOU ALLOWED ME TO NOTIFY THE MAIN FORCE OF THIS CASTLE'S LOCATION. THANKS FOR THAT.
YOU SONU-VA...
WHOA! NO NEED FOR THAT.
WE ENDED UP SAVING YOUR LIFE. COULDN'T YOU AT LEAST SAY THANKS, TOO?

*DMDMDMDM
TURN UP LATER AND I'LL SEE YOU GET BONUS MONEY FOR DISTINGUISHED SERVICE.
YOU KIND OF CREATED A DISTRACTION SO WE COULD BREAK IN.
TCH!
THIS MAKES US EVEN!
SHUT UP! I'VE GOT NO TIME FOR THAT RIGHT NOW...

WILL FIND CHITCH ?
ザァ.. アァ.. ァ.. ァ...
*WHSSSSS
WONDER IF THEY WILL.

IT'S UNCERTAIN WHETHER IT WAS REALITY OR A DREAM.
THAT WAS SO LONG AGO, WHEN HE WAS JUST A BOY.
THE BURIED MEMORY OF AN EARLY SPRING DAY.

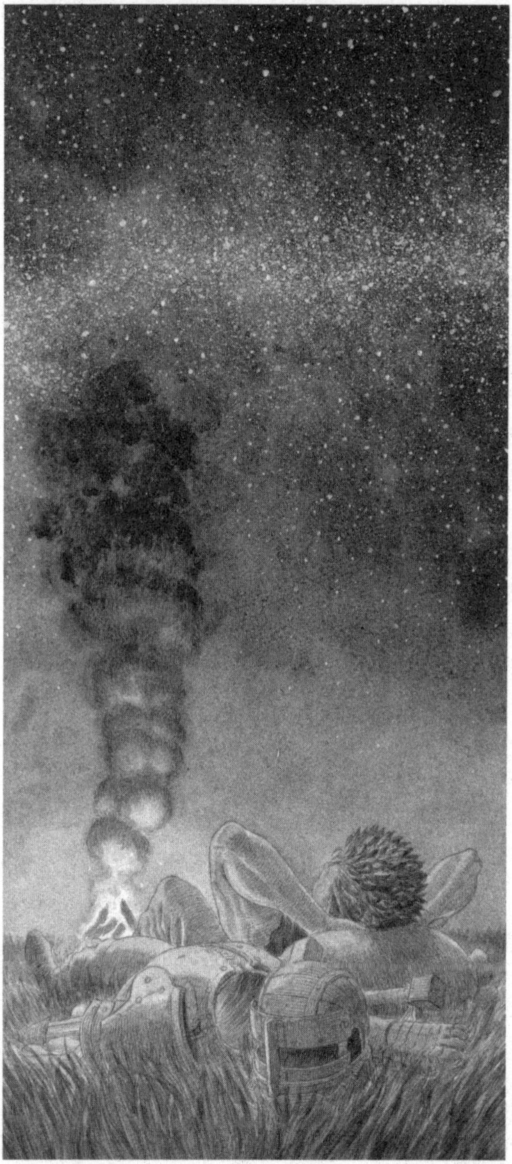

SPRING FLOWERS OF DISTANT DAYS

THE END

幻造世界〈ファンタジア〉篇／妖精島の章

幌馬車

COVERED WAGON

*BRMMM
FASTER!! THEY'RE CATCHIN' UP!!
*ZHA
*ZHA
*ZHA
*ZHA
*ZHA

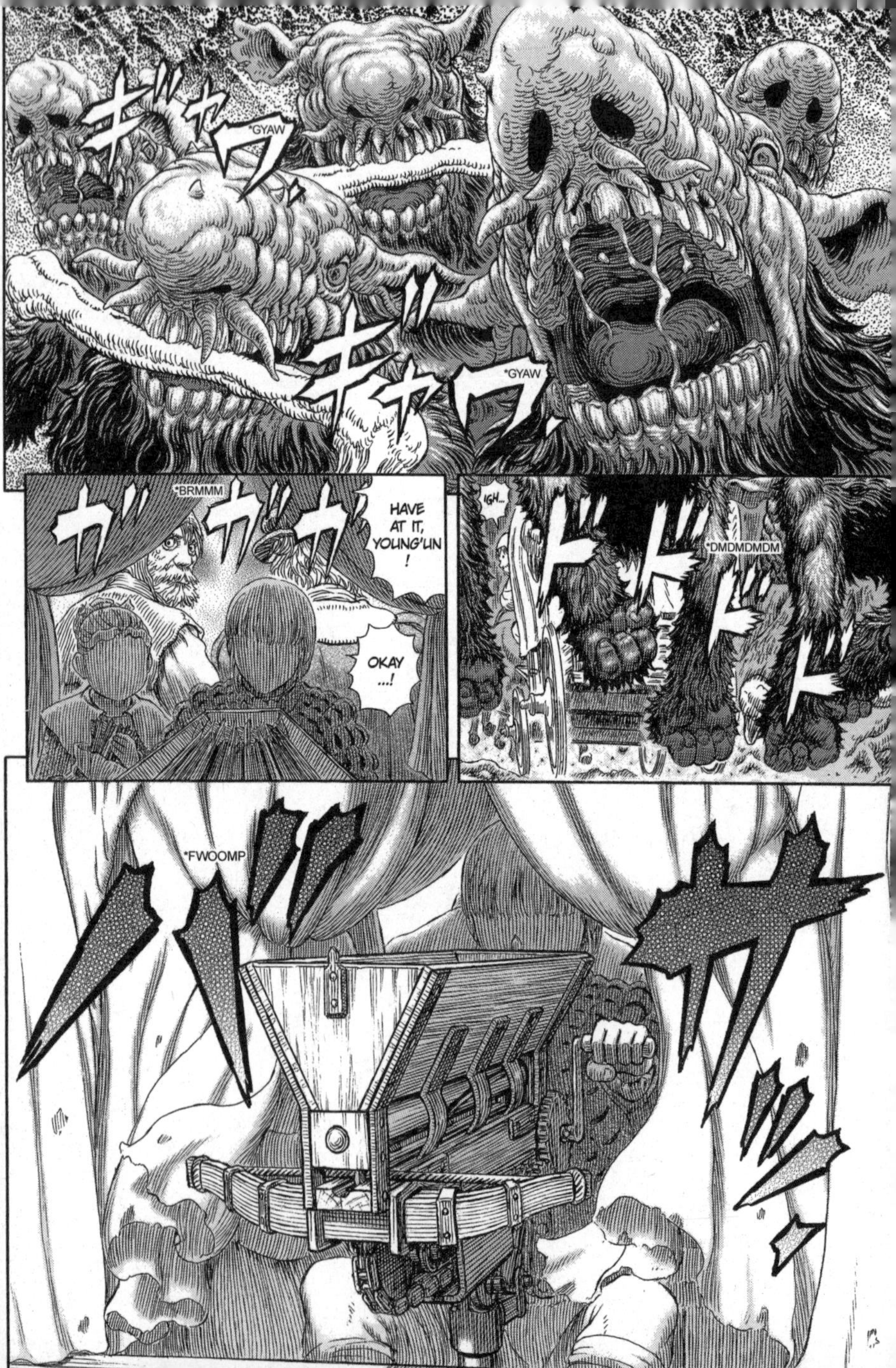
*GYAW
*GYAW
IGH...
*DMDMDMDM
*BRMMM
HAVE AT IT, YOUNG'UN!
OKAY ...!
*FWOOMP

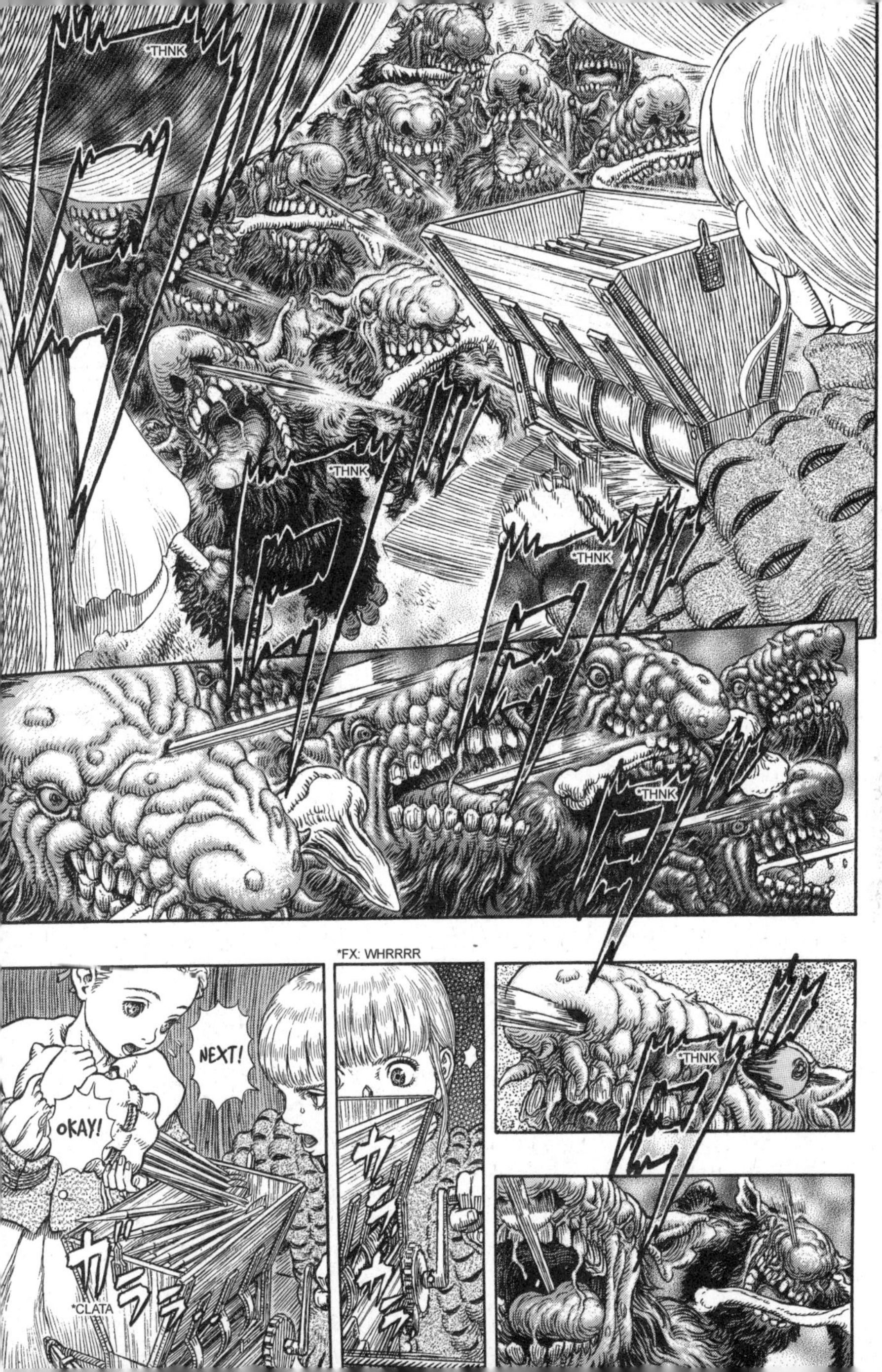

*THNK
*THNK
*THNK
*THNK
*FX: WHRRRR
NEXT!
OKAY!
*CLATA
*THNK

*THMP
*THMP
*THMP
THERE'RE FAR MORE THAN I CAN KILL! GO FASTER!
*CLATA
*CLATA
*THNK
*THNK
*THNK
*FX: CLATA CLATA
WE CAN'T!
THE TWO WAGONS UP FRONT ARE WEIGHED DOWN WITH FOLKS...!
BUT THE BOW-STRING WON'T LAST MUCH--

C-CRAP ...!
*ZHA
*ZHA
*ZHA
*ZHA
*BOING
ERICA, BE CARE-FUL...!
RAGHHH!
O-OH, YEAH! THESE!
*TUNK
*TUNK
*FLING
*GYAWWW
*CHSHHH

*LEAP
*LEAP
*LEAP
*CLATA
*CLATA
AWWW, IT DIDN'T WORK.
THAT WAS TOO DANGER-OUS!
ALL IT DID WAS GIVE US A SMALL LEAD.
THEY'LL CATCH RIGHT UP AGAIN.
S-STOP! STOP!
!
A ROTTED TREE'S BLOCKING THE WAY!
HERE THEY COME-- HERE THEY COME!
*GHEE
*GHEE
*GHEE
ERICA, GET BACK!
*RMMMB

ギリリ
*GRRRN
*VNNN
うわああ
*AUGHHHH
*THNK
*THNK
*THNK
ARROWS RAINED DOWN?!
FROM WHERE?
HEY, LOOK!
!
*DM
*DM
*DM
*DM

*DM
*DM
THAT'S...
THAT FLAG IS...

ALL FORCES, SPREAD OUT LEFT AND RIGHT! INTERCEPT THOSE TROLLS!
*DM
*DM
*DM

*BDADUMP
*BDADUMP
*BDADUMP
*ZHASH
*SHWOP

ARE THOSE...
...MIDLAND KNIGHTS?!
*ROHHHH
I'M SURE OF IT!
THAT WINGED SWORD INSIGNIA ON THEIR FLAG! WHAT'S THEIR NAME...?
Y'KNOW!
OH, RIGHT! THE BAND OF THE HAWK...!
THE WHITE HAWK GRIFFITH LEADS 'EM! IT'S THEIR FLAG!
*GYAHH
*GYAHH
*GYAHH
*ZHA
*ZHA
*ZHA
*ZHA
*ZHA
DON'T PURSUE THEM TOO FAR!
WE NEED TO ESCORT THESE REFUGEES BACK SAFELY!
B-BE CARE-FUL BACK THERE!
!

THERE IS STILL SOMETHING MONSTROUS ON THE PROWL!
*DOOSH
*DOOSH
*KRAKK

RAWWWWK

A COCKA-TRICE ?!
*HRHRHRNN
*PUFF
*PUFF
*GLARE
*FX: FROTH
*BWOOOOF
*SHANNNG
!

C-CAN'T MOVE...
*HOWK
IGHHHH
*HOWK
*FX: CHOMP
IGH!
*HYNN
*ZOSH
ARE YOU ALRIGHT ?!
*GSHANG
*KREEEEE
*PWOF
WHA ?!

*CHFF
IRVINE!
*TUG

*SHOOM
*BWOOOF
UWAH!
*BWOOOSH
EVERY ONE FALL BACK!
DON'T BREATHE ANY OF THAT!

IRVINE!
LOOK AFTER THIS FOR ME.
*FWMP
*VNNN
*GLARE
*FWOOSH

*BROARRR
YOU ARE MY PREY.
*WOOSH
YOU WON'T ESCAPE.

...!
ザワ ザワ
*SHFFFF
THAT'S A...!!
ギリリ...
*KRRRN

*VNNG

B E S E R K

幻造世界〈ファンタジア〉篇／妖精島の章

楽土

PARADISE

*DOOOOSH
ズズウウン

*ROHHHHH
IRVINE!
IRVINE THE ARCANE ARCHER!
WOW!
HE BROUGHT DOWN THAT GIANT CHICKEN WITH A SINGLE ARROW!
IS HE A MONSTER ...? MAYBE A MONSTER MAN?
LOOKS LIKE HE'S WITH THE KNIGHTS,
AND HE SAVED US...
WHAT IS THIS...?
SO THE DEER MAN'S ON OUR SIDE, RIGHT?

WHAT'S GOING...
...ON HERE...?!
YOU KNOW, I'VE HEARD PEOPLE TALKIN'.
THEY SAY THE HAWK DOESN'T JUST LEAD HUMANS. HE EVEN HAS AN ARMY OF SCARY MONSTERS.
I RECKONED THAT WAS ALL BULL, BUT NOW...
*CHFF

WHOA, WHOA!
TH-THAT WAS SCARY, RICKERT.
RICKERT ?
...
*HRHRRNN

WHAT IN THE WORLD HAPPENED...?
GRIFFITH ?
IT'S NOT EVEN BUDGING.
WE NEED MORE HELP...
*FX: CLAK
!
*SHOVE
*DOOSH
GOOD! EVERYONE, MOVE OUT!

*CLATA
*CLATA
*CLATA
*CLATA
THERE WE GO.
*FX: PUSH
WHEW!
WELL, THAT'S A RELIEF.
...
...
...
THAT DAY, ON THE HILL OF SWORDS...
...RIGHT IN FRONT OF ME AND GUTS...
...GRIFFITH FLEW AWAY, RIDING ON ZODD THE IMMORTAL.

HE WAS DIFFERENT SOMEHOW, FROM THE GRIFFITH WE KNEW...
AND YET, HE SEEMED MORE GRIFFITH... IT WAS A STRANGE IMPRESSION.
I HEARD TALES ON THE WIND THAT DURING THE KUSHAN INVASION, THE HAWK WAS ONCE AGAIN LEADING THE BAND OF THE HAWK AND FIGHTING TO LIBERATE MIDLAND.
HONESTLY, I OFTEN CONSIDERED RUNNING OFF TO SEE.
HEY, ARE YOU OKAY? YOU LOOK PALE.
I'M FINE...
REALLY ?
BUT NOW I HAVE SOMETHING I WANT TO PROTECT...
...HOWEVER, ...
THINGS HAVE CHANGED SINCE THEN...
IN MIDLAND...
NO, IN THE WORLD.

*FLAP
*FLAP
*FLAP
*GACHIK
*FX: GYAHHH
HMMM ...
ギャアアアア!
!
*THNK
*THNK
*THNK

*WHEWWW
WH-WHAT'S UP? WERE THERE MORE OF 'EM?!
GOT 'EM!
MAYBE THERE'S NOWHERE...
...LEFT IN THE WORLD WHERE HUMANS CAN LIVE IN SAFETY.
*FX: CLOP CLOP
THAT WAS IMPRES-SIVE.
PRETTY GREAT, HUH?!
IS THAT CROSSBOW YOURS, THEN?
*GCHAK
NOW I SEE... THE FACT THAT THIS GROUP GOT THIS FAR SAFELY MUST BE LARGELY THANKS TO YOU AND THAT WEAPON.
... ...!
ARE YOU...
...GENERAL LABAN?

MY NAME IS RICKERT.
A MEMBER OF THE FORMER BAND OF THE HAWK.
YES, AND YOU ARE...?
I SAW YOU SEVERAL TIMES ON THE BATTLEFIELD DURING THE HUNDRED-YEARS WAR.
*FX: RUMMAGE
I AM...
UMM...
THEN YOU WERE ONE OF THE HEROES WHO SAVED THE KINGDOM.
WELL, WELL...
THE HUNDRED-YEARS WAR... THAT FEELS LIKE THE DISTANT PAST NOW.
...IT DOES.
SO MUCH SO, THAT IT MAKES...
...THE TIME WHEN NATIONS AND PEOPLE...
...FOUGHT EACH OTHER SEEM DOWNRIGHT TRANQUIL.
SINCE THEN, OUR KINGDOM...
...NO, THE ***WORLD*** HAS CHANGED CONSIDER-ABLY.

BUT THERE'S NO CALL FOR DESPAIR.
ISN'T THAT...
...THE REASON YOU'VE COME ALL THIS WAY?
WE'VE CLEARED THE FOREST.
!
WHAT'RE THOSE?
THEY'RE CALLED "WING STONES."

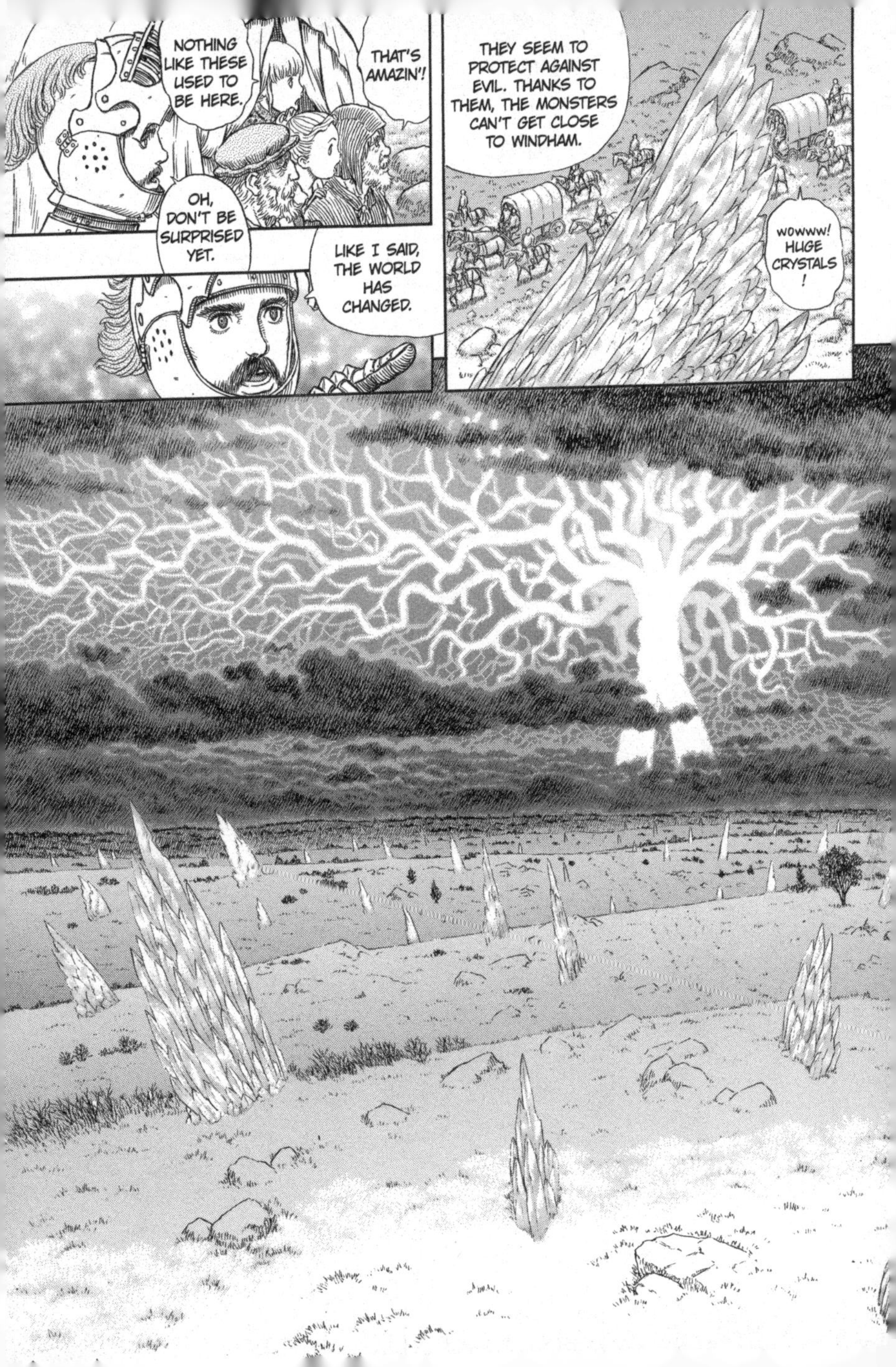
NOTHING LIKE THESE USED TO BE HERE.
THAT'S AMAZIN'!
OH, DON'T BE SURPRISED YET.
LIKE I SAID, THE WORLD HAS CHANGED.
THEY SEEM TO PROTECT AGAINST EVIL. THANKS TO THEM, THE MONSTERS CAN'T GET CLOSE TO WINDHAM.
WOWWW! HUGE CRYSTALS!

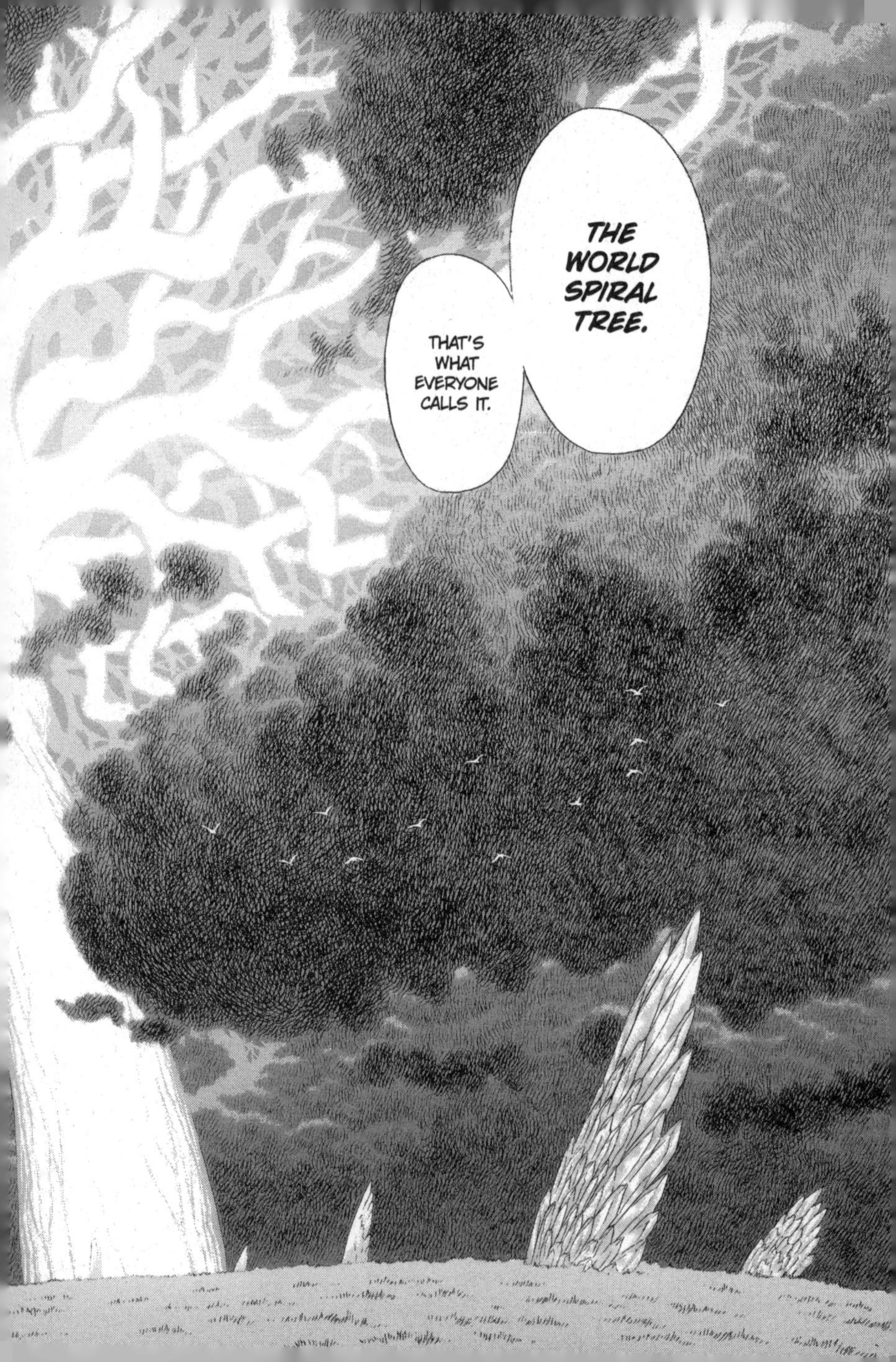
THE WORLD SPIRAL TREE.
THAT'S WHAT EVERYONE CALLS IT.

WHOAAA... IT'S BIIIIG...
Y'THINK MAYBE THOSE LINE-LIKE THINGS THAT SHOW UP IN THE SKY SOMETIMES...
WH-WHAT, THAT THEY'RE THIS THING'S BRANCHES OR SOMETHIN'? BUT A BUNCH OF THOSE THINGS GO CLEAR OVER MOUNTAINS.

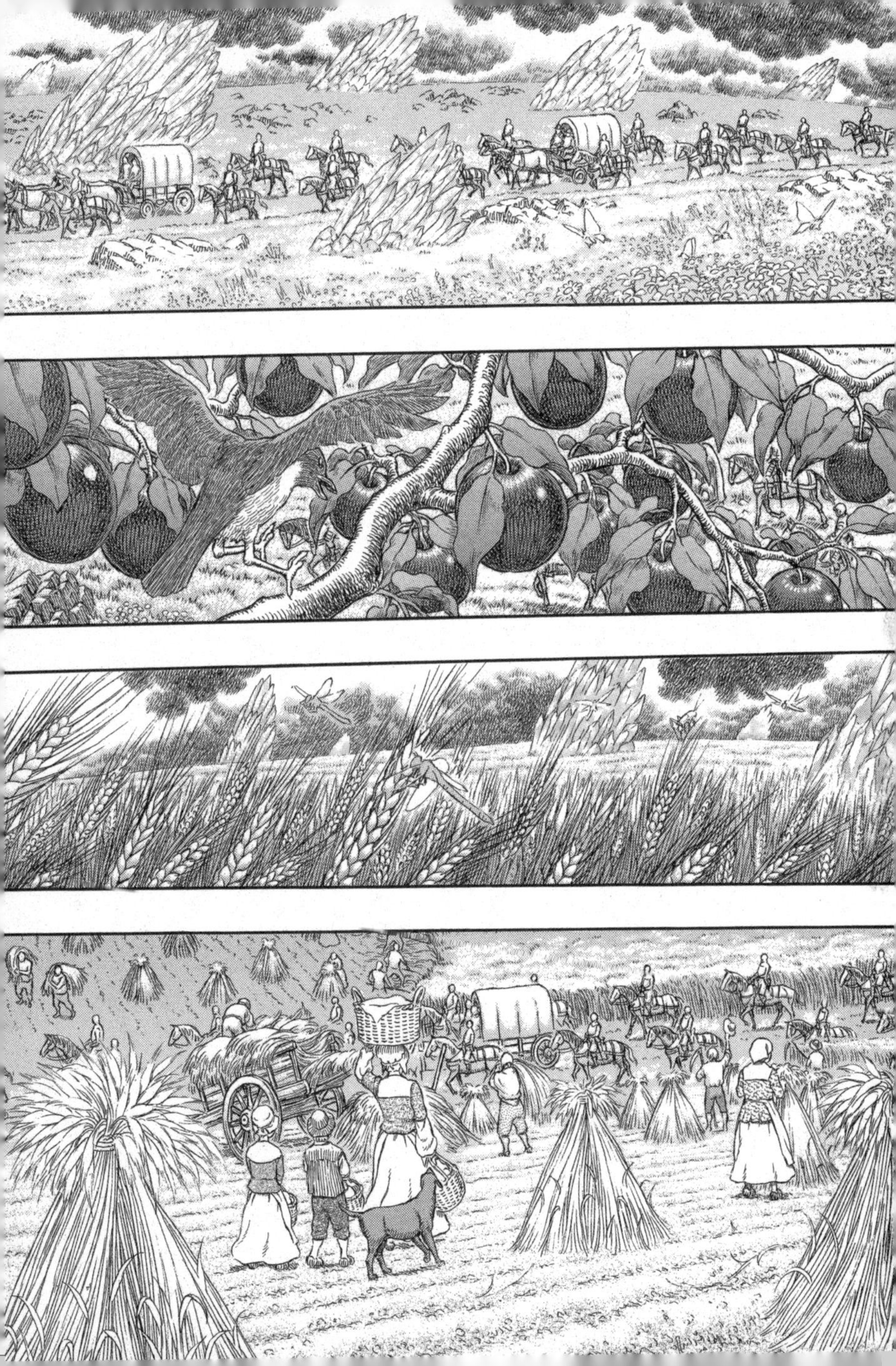

WOW! THIS PLACE IS SO PRETTY!
IT-IT'S HARD TO BELIEVE THERE'S SO MANY PEOPLE...JUST WORKIN'.
EVERY TOWN AND VILLAGE WE SAW ON THE WAY HERE HAD BEEN ROUGHED UP BAD BY THEM MONSTERS...
IT'S NOT JUST THAT.
IT'S EARLY SPRING RIGHT NOW, YET LOOK AT ALL THOSE HEADS OF GRAIN.
YEAH, YOU'RE RIGHT...
CURRENTLY IN THE AREA AROUND WINDHAM, HARVEST SEASON NEVER ENDS FOR FLOWERS, TREES, AND GRAINS.
I DON'T KNOW THE REASON, BUT EVERYONE BELIEVES IT'S BECAUSE THE WORLD SPIRAL TREE BLESSES US.
THANKS TO THAT...
LOOK.
WINDHAM...
I MEAN...

... FALCONIA ...
...IS ABLE TO TAKE IN ALL THOSE REFUGEES.

FALCONIA...

IT'S THE SOLE STRONGHOLD IN THIS WORLD WHERE PEOPLE...
...CAN LIVE THEIR LIVES *AS* PEOPLE.

BERSERK

STOP

This is the back of the book!

This manga collection is translated into English but oriented in right-to-left reading format at the creator's request, maintaining the artwork's visual orientation as originally published in Japan. If you've never read manga in this way before, take a look at the diagram below to give yourself an idea of how to go about it. Basically, you'll be starting in the upper right corner and will read each balloon and panel moving right to left. It may take some getting used to, but you should get the hang of it very quickly. Have fun!

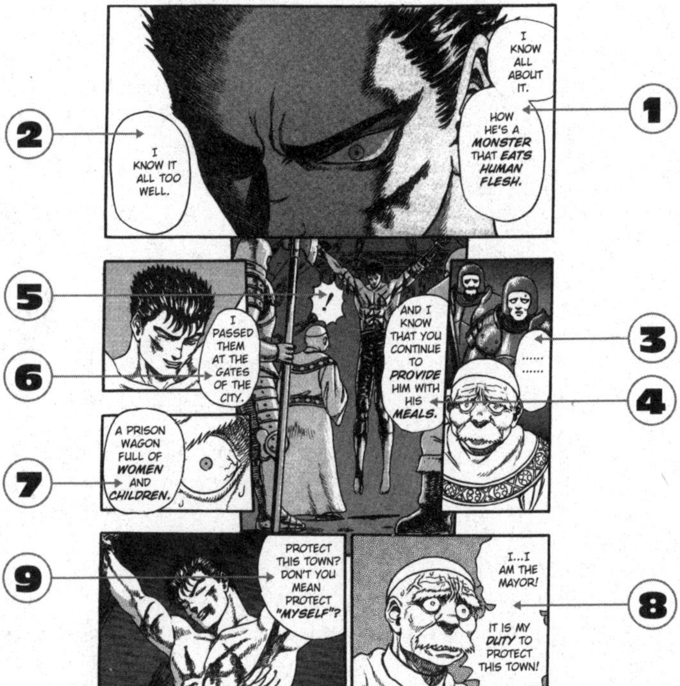

VAMPIRE HUNTER D

HIDEYUKI KIKUCHI | ILLUSTRATIONS BY YOSHITAKA AMANO

From creator Hideyuki Kikuchi, one of Japan's leading horror authors, with illustrations by renowned Japanese artist Yoshitaka Amano, this series is here printed in an English translation for the first time anywhere!

Volume 1
ISBN 978-1-59582-012-9
$11.99

Volume 2:
RAISER OF GALES
ISBN 978-1-59582-014-3
$11.99

Volume 3:
DEMON DEATHCHASE
ISBN 978-1-59582-031-0
$11.99

Volume 4:
TALE OF THE DEAD TOWN
ISBN 978-1-59582-093-8
$9.99

Volume 5:
THE STUFF OF DREAMS
ISBN 978-1-59582-094-5
$8.99

Volume 6:
PILGRIMAGE OF THE SACRED AND THE PROFANE
ISBN 978-1-59582-106-5
$9.99

Volume 7:
MYSTERIOUS JOURNEY TO THE NORTH SEA PART ONE
ISBN 978-1-59582-107-2
$8.99

Volume 8:
MYSTERIOUS JOURNEY TO THE NORTH SEA PART TWO
ISBN 978-1-59582-108-9
$8.99

Volume 9:
THE ROSE PRINCESS
ISBN 978-1-59582-109-6
$8.99

Volume 10:
DARK NOCTURNE
ISBN 978-1-59582-132-4
$8.99

Volume 11:
PALE FALLEN ANGEL PARTS ONE AND TWO
ISBN 978-1-59582-130-0
$14.99

Volume 12:
PALE FALLEN ANGEL PARTS THREE AND FOUR
ISBN 978-1-59582-131-7
$14.99

Volume 13:
TWIN-SHADOWED KNIGHT PARTS ONE AND TWO
ISBN 978-1-59307-930-7
$14.99

Volume 14:
DARK ROAD PARTS ONE AND TWO
ISBN 978-1-59582-440-0
$14.99

Volume 15:
DARK ROAD PART THREE
ISBN 978-1-59582-500-1
$9.99

Volume 16:
TYRANT'S STARS PARTS ONE AND TWO
ISBN 978-1-59582-572-8
$14.99

Volume 17:
TYRANT'S STARS PARTS THREE AND FOUR
ISBN 978-1-59582-820-0
$14.99

Volume 18:
FORTRESS OF THE ELDER GOD
ISBN 978-1-59582-976-4
$10.99

Volume 19:
MERCENARY ROAD
ISBN 978-1-61655-073-8
$11.99

Volume 20:
SCENES FROM AN UNHOLY WAR
ISBN 978-1-61655-255-8
$11.99

Volume 21:
RECORD OF THE BLOOD BATTLE
ISBN 978-1-61655-437-8
$11.99

Volume 22:
WHITE DEVIL MOUNTAIN PARTS ONE AND TWO
ISBN 978-1-61655-509-2
$11.99

Volume 23:
IRIYA THE BERSERKER
ISBN 978-1-61655-706-5
$11.99

Volume 24:
THRONG OF HERETICS
ISBN 978-1-61655-789-8
$11.99

Volume 25:
UNDEAD ISLAND
ISBN 978-1-50670-163-9
$11.99

Volume 26:
BEDEVILED STAGECOACH
ISBN 978-1-50670-199-8
$11.99

Volume 27:
NIGHTMARE VILLAGE
ISBN 978-1-50670-927-7
$11.99

AVAILABLE AT YOUR LOCAL COMICS SHOP OR BOOKSTORE

To find a comics shop near you, visit comicshoplocator.com • For more information or to order direct: On the web: DarkHorse.com • E-mail: mailorder@DarkHorse.com • Phone: 1-800-862-0052 Mon.–Fri. 9 AM to 5 PM Pacific Time.